Witl

MW00767902

The Deadly Reef

CORBETT A. DAVIS JR.

Baltimore, Maryland

The Deadly Reef

Chapter illustrations by Bill Hinton

Library of Congress
Cataloging in Publication Data
ISBN 1-56167-554-7

Library of Congress Card Catalog Number:
99-66264

Published by

Noble House

8019 Belair Road, Suite 10
Baltimore, Maryland 21236

Manufactured in the United States of America

Dedication

For my son Corbett III,
who always makes me proud and keeps me smiling.

ACKNOWLEDGMENTS

I have many friends I would like to thank for helping this fly fishing jeweler complete his first attempt at a book.

To John Cole, a fine gentleman, great writer and valued friend, thanks for your faith and encouragement.

To Jimbo Meador of Point Clear Alabama and Fuzzy Davis of Hilton Head South Carolina, I cherish your friendship and great stories. I also appreciate the introduction to Captain Limbo.

To all the folks at Deep Water Cay Bonefish Lodge, especially Walter Mon, thanks for the Fun Times chasing bones.

Although ya'll make it tough to stay slim Gracias to Carlos, Flora, Noa, and Denise at Coco's Cantina on Cudjoe Key. Nobody can cook it like you.

To Ronnetha Ryals who helped me slightly more than she cussed me as she transferred my scribbles to the computer.

And lastly thanks to Dad, who has taught me everything I know about fishing, conservation, business, and making it in this life. Thanks to my mother for teaching me how to enjoy it all.

FOREWORD

Corbett tells a good story, but there is more to this book. Like every good novel, it will involve you, put you right there with Powell Taylor as he gets more and more involved with adventures that may cost him his life.

But as you read, you'll learn as much about south Florida as you do about Powell and his high-risk encounters. For what, in my opinion, is best about this lively book is the author's knowledge and understanding of the places he writes about.

There are all too many of us who picture south Florida and most of the state, for that matter, as a combination of Disneyland, Miami Vice, and orange juice. We are deluged with direct-mail four-color come-ons trying to sell us a piece of the palm trees and frost-free winters. Over the years, even if we do visit the place every now and then, we begin to see Florida as a kind of Never-Never Land where bikinis are the uniform of the day and margaritas the official state beverage.

Which, of course, is not the way it is, not at all. But given the amount of high-pressure hype that keeps coming our way, getting a chance to know the real Florida becomes more and more difficult. Until you read Corbett's book.

Because it's written by a guy who is Florida-born and Florida-raised and who loves his native state, this is a book that can enlighten and teach all of us a great deal about a Florida most of us will never see. Even if we traveled the same roads as Powell Taylor, we wouldn't see as much as he does because we wouldn't know what to look for, not until we'd read this book.

Which is important, because until we do know what to look for, we'll never see the Florida that's really there, the place where Corbett Davis Jr., was born and raised, where his father was born and where Corbett III is starting his career as a Florida man.

Novelist Lawrence Durrell, whose trilogy transports us to the Middle East, once wrote an essay about the importance of "a sense of place." Each of us, he wrote, has a home landscape in his mind's eye, a place we return to in our dreams, a place that is our home. Few, if any, of the trendy south Florida novelists of the day can match this book's sense of place. Which, to my way of thinking, is one of the very best reasons for reading it. And along the way, you'll discover a bang-up story and a hero you just have to like.

—John N. Cole

Prologue

I awoke to a burning sensation on my weathered back, an uncomfortable and unfamiliar dizziness surrounded my brain. It took a few moments to collect my thoughts, remove the fog from my mind and realize just where I was: adrift alone in a small raft in what appeared to be a very large ocean. Looking down at my arms, chest, and legs I knew from their dark, leathery appearance I must have had a hell of a vacation in the sun. "No, this can't be a vacation. I feel too bad," I thought aloud.

As I talked to myself, my mind wandered off, picturing a tired old Hemingway afloat in his novel, questioning his sanity as he talked to the fish, wondering if he would ever see his only friend, the young boy. Stop! I thought—Make yourself think, survive, stay alive, Jimmy Buffett. No wait, make yourself figure out where on earth you are and how you got here. The dark, rich blue of the water told me I was well offshore, the Gulf Stream possibly. A cold Corona with a slice of key lime would be good about now, maybe with some black beans, yellow rice, and a fried slab of fresh grouper. Better yet, maybe I'll float up on some primitive island with hundreds of miles of flats, never before seen by humans. Nothing but huge schools of bonefish and permit in the water, and dark-skinned ladies ashore, ready to accommodate, plenty of vacancies. Once again I told myself I must think, think hard. I wasn't sure why these notions were popping into my thoughts. I knew I was a long way from home, and quite certain I was nowhere near Gulf Breeze, Florida. It seemed as if a lifetime had passed since I visited the panhandle of my childhood and the safe community where I grew up. Let's see now—The Gulf Stream, Hemingway, Buffett, Key Limes, Cuban food, bonefish. Ah yes, it's all coming back, the end of the rainbow, mile marker zero, the southernmost point ninety miles from Cuba and, of course, gorgeous sunsets. I'm somewhere near latitude 24. 6, Key West Florida.

Fading in and out of reality as the sun slipped away, my memory slowly returned sending small bumps up the back of my spine. As I tried to get as comfortable as possible in a two-man rubber raft, I laid back and began reliving the past, hoping that I would soon be sipping mass quantities of frozen blender magic from some balcony on Duval Street.

Chapter One

When people would ask why I love the Keys, no answer seemed to fit. How does one explain the Gulf Stream to someone who has never ridden it? No description of a sunset over Key West Harbor can be appropriate to someone who has never seen it. How do you describe the jesters and minstrels who entertain nightly at Key West's Mallory Square for an audience that always shows up? Neither rain squalls, small craft warnings nor even hurricane threats can squelch the never routine party that ends each day in this colorful paradise where the Atlantic meets the Gulf of Mexico.

The Keys are not a location, not real estate, not just a place on the map. They are an attitude, a way of life.

They represent the best memories of my youth. In the early years my mother and father struggled to make ends meet. My father, Charles P. Taylor, Sr., decided at an early age not to follow his family's suggestions. They thought he should work for the railroad while the money was good. He had other dreams and ideas of his own. He and my mother, Imogene worked hard together to learn what they needed to open their own retail jewelry store. My father apprenticed with some of the finest jewelers in the South, while my mother learned all she could about bookkeeping. They both grew up in Mobile, Alabama, but moved to Pensacola just before I was born. I was always glad of that. When people ask me where I'm from, Florida always seems a better reply than Alabama.

By my fourth birthday, I had a younger brother, Brad. By the time I was ten, our parents had opened "Taylors Fine Jewelry" in Gulf Breeze, Florida. It seems as if they worked thousands of hours a week building their dream. Brad and I would help out with sweeping floors or cleaning showcases. By age eleven, I had mastered the engraving machine and was responsible for all of the store's engraving jobs. About this time in my life I began wondering whether or not the jewelry business was really my future. Although I was the oldest son, I never pictured myself as the serious business type.

When I turned fifteen, the pressures of retailing eased up and our family began to take real vacations, not the business trips of earlier years when we traveled the South and hit every town that had even a small jewelry store. While my mother, I and my brother sat in the car, Dear Old Dad would talk to every store owner and convince them to let him do their jewelry repairs and custom work. After five years of this, he had more than one hundred accounts. From small, home-owned jewelry stores to large chains, he always kept them happy. But it was those vacations later in life that left such lasting memories. No matter how hectic life might be, we would take off the first two weeks of July. The diamond cutters, the jewelry manufacturers and the gold refineries in New York closed those two weeks.

Mom and Dad would start counting our vacation votes in June, but we always ended up on US 1, headed south. When we hit Key Largo, life slowed its feverish pace. The sun shone brighter, the air got a tad crisper and the ocean turned crystal clear. There were no deadlines, no customers, no arguments and no stress. We were a real family with nary a worry. In the years to come these were the days Mom and Dad often would refer to as "The Good Old Days." The older I got the wiser they got, and they damn well may have been right on this one.

With my degree in Business Management from Florida State

University, I returned home with plans of running the family business. During the almost five years it took me to complete my courses at FSU, I could count on one hand the number of weekends I spent there. Most of the other students joined fraternities or sororities, fished or enjoyed picnics, or just flat out partied every weekend. But by three o'clock every Friday afternoon I was on highway 20 headed for Gulf Breeze. I worked every Saturday building character and learning the retail business. So I was told. Between this and the knowledge I gained from the classroom I knew all the answers.

The year after I returned home, I continued studying and working hard. I became one of the only three certified gemologists in the area. My diploma from the California-based Gemological Institute of America read Charles P. Taylor, Jr. However, everyone at GIA and in my hometown of Gulf Breeze knew me simply as Powell Taylor. Using my middle name gave me a separate identity from Charles P. Sr.

My father had pushed me hard and coached me well. And although I never questioned his motives or why I spent those years training as a gemologist, I was soon to discover just how valuable that knowledge could be. With my knowledge of gemstones came much pleasure. I was fascinated not only with the beauty, rarity and durability of gems, but also with the romance and history they possess.

The early Greeks and Romans adorned them for their medicinal values as well as for the supernatural powers they contain. Charles Sr. had a gift of using those mystical powers to his advantage.

"Use the information from all the past centuries to interest and educate the public. Sell tradition," he would say.

I spent thousands of hours learning that tradition. I knew that sapphires and rubies were blue and red variations of the same stone. I knew the entire mystique that surrounds most of the twenty or so more important gems. It was interesting to me that of the two thousand minerals that have been identified, only ninety or so have varieties that produce specimens of beauty and durability to be considered gemstones. And of these ninety, only about twenty are particularly important to the jeweler.

I knew about all of the birthstones and why they were chosen. I knew that my favorite birthstone, emerald, was chosen as the birthstone for May to symbolize the beauty and promise of nature that spring brought each year. Long ago, the Romans dedicated the emerald to the goddess Venus. It represented faith, kindness, and goodness. It was these same qualities that my mother had helped me realize were most important in this life.

All of this knowledge is like a lot of the stuff we learn over the years. We don't always realize how handy it can be until the day we need it. And for Charles Powell, Jr. that day would come sooner than he imagined.

At twenty-three, I realized it was time to make some major decisions. I'd been in love about fifteen different times, once seriously. But it was not to be; we parted ways. She blamed the business for taking up too much of my time. I blamed her for wasting my time. I needed space. She gave it to me when she moved to Seattle with a Seiko salesman who used to stay with me when he was in town. I thought about dropping the Seiko line and picking up Timex. John Cameron Swayze would have agreed that his watch and I had a lot in common — "Takes a lickin and keeps on tickin'."

I was quickly approaching Charles Sr.'s second phase of his philosophy of life. He taught us that the first twenty-five years are for schooling and preparing you for what you will do. The second twenty-five years you do what you have prepared yourself for. The third twenty-five are for kicking back and enjoying the benefits of what you accomplished in your first fifty years.

So far, I'd done exactly what Charles Sr. wanted me to do. I was pissed at him for manipulating my life. I was pissed at women in general for some reason I wasn't sure of and I hoped that Mr. Bulova would come back and beat the shit out of Mr. Seiko. It was time for a change.

What was the reason for the gravitational tug that was drawing me closer to the equator? It was a combination of all those good memories of trips with my family to the Keys. And in my spare time, I read books that took me south. I helped Hemingway boat many a marlin in Cuba. I was aboard Travis McGee's houseboat, the Busted Flush in every one of John D. MacDonald's adventures.

I watched as Travis and Meyer moved from island to island salvaging people's lives for monies that enabled them to fish and enjoy life. I poled the Key West flats in search of tarpon and permit in Tom McGuane's *Ninety-Two in The Shade*. I listened to Buffett music paint pictures of islands and palms that stayed forever in my mind. I was ready to change latitudes.

I was ready to take a ride on the *FUJIMO*, a forty-eight foot Hatteras yacht I'd seen in Destin one night. I asked the owner, who was also the captain, just what did the name *FUJIMO* mean. He stared me down and said, "Fuck you Jack I'm moving on." He turned and walked away. It took me a couple of seconds to realize he wasn't being a jerk, but just answering my question! It was time for me to move on. FUJIMO!

Abandoning my previous life was not an easy decision. Leaving the comfortable, predestined retail life behind caused me more than a month of sleepless nights. It had always seemed to be a no-way-out situation. I hoped my father would understand now what his father had learned to live with over the years. Just as he preferred not to work for his dad and the railroad, I had to pursue my own dreams. Our family was a close-knit bunch with a house full of love. Mom and Dad worked hard to provide us with everything we needed. Although brother Brad and I had the usual brotherly brawls, we managed to grow up closer than any two brothers I know. To this day, if anyone dares to make an unfavorable remark about Brad, I'm in their face. He's the same way. My mother is a great person who manages to keep everyone happy. Being a tad more spiritual and religious than the rest of us, she saw to it that we had a good Catholic upbringing. Brad and I had twelve years of Catholic education, served as altar boys for six years and knew the mass in both Latin and English.

Every Sunday morning my mother would take my younger brother and me to St. Anne's Cathedral before five a.m. Named the Fisherman's Mass, the five-thirty service was my favorite. Originally it was provided for the fisherman who needed an early start on the water. For me, it was a way to please my mother while not wasting away the whole day. Dressed in her best Sunday dress, Mom would sit in the very front pew waiting for her two "holy" sons to assist Father Gallagher in worship of the mass. In those days women always wore hats or head coverings in church. It must have been some kind of church law.

From my place at the side of the altar I would often glance across the large congregation of mostly women; the assortment of head dress always amused me in those most solemn moments. Father Gallagher would be dressed in his finest robes. Brad and I wore immaculately ironed white surplice and black cassocks. The smell of incense filled the church as the colorful display of sunlight beamed through the stained glass windows. Father held his arms high to the heavens. I rang the ceremonial bells and brother Brad laughed aloud. I looked across the altar in his direction to see a huge grin, wondering just what had tickled him at this moment. Was it the communion wine we had sneaked a taste of earlier before mass? Perhaps it was the very overweight lady in the third row with a lacy doily pinned to the top of her newly fixed Sunday bouffant that created his laughter.

I'm not exactly sure when it was no longer considered reverent for the ladies to cover their heads, but the last time I visited a mass, I only saw one hat. The Catholic church has changed with the times, I guess. Overall, I am happy with the changes. The mass makes much more sense to me in English than it ever did in Latin. However, I feel that some needed reverence was lost when the Pope decided to replace the "Mea Culpa" with the English translation of Have Mercy. No longer having to abstain from eating meat on Fridays also pleased me. But I did worry about all those poor Catholic souls who were sent to Purgatory for sneaking a Big Mac on Friday night after work. I also wonder how long it will be before priests are allowed to marry. Tradition in Imogene Taylor's church is being lost forever. Although she never said so, Mom was probably a little disappointed.

In grammar school, I went to confession every Friday. Once, as a fifth grader, I was nervous about confession, not because I was afraid to confess my sins, but because I couldn't think of any sins that I had actually committed since the last Friday. I finally got out the ten commandments and started confessing to some of the lesser ones. "Bless me Father, for I have sinned, it's been seven whole days since my last confession. Father, I've lied to my teacher twice, I stole my brother's lunch money once and I committed adultery three times." I remember a slight chuckle coming from the tight-lipped mouth above the Roman collar looking down at me.

"Son for your penance I want you to tell the truth, return your brother's money and say twenty Hail Marys."

"Yes Father," I said ever so reverently.

"Oh and son, try to cut back on the adultery."

"Yes Father!"

"Piece of cake," I thought. This confession was great. I felt like a new man. My sins were gone and I was forgiven. My soul was white as snow. My life went so smoothly I used the same sins for the next four Fridays.

One day after school my mother waited for me at the bus stop. We walked the five blocks home. "Father Gallagher called me today," she said. By the time she got through explaining adultery, I was confused. But I was sure of one thing; I damn well never adultered anyone. Next Friday I would confess to making up sins to confess.

Mom was great! Dad was great! Brother Brad was great! Then why was I about to leave all of this behind to follow some crazy-ass dream of mine? Nepotism didn't seem to fit my realm of thought at the moment. Later it might, but for now I had to move on. I was on a similar course with that Destin Hatteras.

Chapter Two

I remember the day I left like it was this morning. We all awoke early and walked out on the dock to talk. As we were saying our goodbyes, I noticed a large school of mullet churning the surface of the water less than fifty yards away. Right in our own back yard was a watery wonderment of wildlife so typical of the most unique coast line in all of the fifty states. Here, only twenty miles from the Alabama line we were blessed with living at the beginning of a magical coast. As I watched the large outline of feeding mullet cross a shallow sand bar, I remembered something of great importance. I had forgotten to pack my cast net. I learned to throw a net at the early age of six. My father had much more patience in those days. He showed me the proper way to coil the thirty feet of line in my left hand, while holding the lead line between my teeth and the other half of monofilament meshing in my right hand. He watched and coached as I practiced day and night. Finally, when I could manage to open up the net three out of four casts on the living room floor, Dad decided it was time to take his student to the water.

Catching my first mullet was a memory that can never be

matched. Feeling that first bump against the side of my net created a sensation that is hard to explain.

Charles, Sr. helped me with every step of my first net-caught fish. We scaled him, removed his head and filleted him out. As my grandfather used to say, "We ate everything but his lips and his asshole." We fried the filets, the backbone and even his gizzard. It was the sweetest fish I would ever eat.

I ran up to the house grabbed my cast net and returned at the perfect time. The school was just coming into casting range. With one throw I had about twenty fish.

I kept six frying size ones and released the others. It was a great farewell breakfast. Brad and I cleaned the fish while Dad cranked up his butane cooker and Mom made grits and coffee. Charles Sr. started to get a little aggravated because we only had white cornmeal and no yellow. He must have thought about it and realized that on this day it was a minor thing.

Eating our fresh breakfast on the end of the wharf, watching as gulls and terns dove down and picked the mullet bellies from the surface of the slick bay, we counted ten different species of feeding birds, from pelicans, laughing gulls, herring gulls, ring-billed gulls and Forsters terns to one great blue heron that came flying down and landed in water about three feet deeper than he'd estimated. He looked awkward kicking his feet, swimming like a wounded duck with his unwebbed digits only inches from the bottom. None of us had ever seen a blue heron swim before.

The laughter ended when I announced it was time for me to leave. Although I was heading just eight hundred fifty miles away from our home in Gulf Breeze, it seemed as if I was moving to another country. I wasn't even leaving the state, just changing ends.

Florida's twenty-one million acres of forests, lakes, marshes and beaches has so many areas with natural vitality, it is slow to surrender to the developers and the bulldozers that have ruined so many other coastal states. Cities throughout Florida, such as Gulf Breeze, are still undiscovered paradises. I hoped that life in the Keys would bring as much pleasure as I had known growing up in north Florida. There would soon be times when I questioned my move to the southern-most point of Florida.

With all the tears of goodbye, I was feeling guilty, even though the jewelry store was doing well, my parents were happy and Brad was engaged. I had no reason to feel bad about leaving. But I did. This guilt thing was not a new feeling. I thought for a moment I should go to confession and confess something. I would feel much better and clean again. I had drifted slightly away from the church in the past few years. I hoped my mother was not angry at me because of it. I hoped my family still loved me in spite of my desertion.

In the rear view mirror I watched as my waving family disappeared into the blue-gray water of the bay that blinked behind them. I did not relish the thought of the eight hundred fifty mile drive ahead of me. Fifteen hours to think about whether I'd made the right decision or not. No, that I would not do. Time to clear the mind and think good thoughts, meditate on happy things with happy endings. I began to think of what I'd brought with me. There was more than a boat, some tackle and clothes. I was bringing everything with me, everything my father had taught me about business, fishing and conservation. I was bringing everything my mother taught me about discipline, religion and having fun. I was bringing all the good times Bradford A. Taylor and his older brother Powell had had together. This would be a happy journey.

By the time I hit Grayton Beach down old Highway 98, I was feeling better. I decided I was in no hurry to reach Key West. Steadily moving east on Highway 98, I watched as the beautiful, serene, sandy beaches became a row of trashy, cheap motels, bowling alleys, go-cart tracks, souvenir shell factories, bars and T-shirt shops. I thought I'd never get past this rape of the land. It took about an hour and twenty minutes to travel the twenty-five-mile tourist strip crowded with late spring-breakers. These vacationing college kids were more fortunate than I when it came to Spring Break. Traveling from different locations all over the south, they were drinking, partying and raising hell. This was a luxury I missed out on in my earlier years.

As I passed Panama City, the highway returned to the beautiful sugar beaches, sand dunes and aqua-blue Gulf waters. My blood pressure dropped about a thousand points. I decided to stop in Apalachicola where I sucked down two dozen raw oysters and a couple of cold drafts. The oysters were just salty enough and ten cents each. In Key West they would be five dollars a dozen and probably taste just adequate, at best. I drove up toward Tallahassee and decided to stay the night at Wakulla Springs. The weathered wood frame buildings nestled in a colorful old Florida setting with crystal clear springs with a perfect old cabin that was my bunkhouse.

Wakulla Springs must be home for about a thousand different species of birds. I was up early and by eight-thirty I had eaten breakfast and taken both the river cruise and the glass-bottom boat ride. Among the birds I saw along the way were a purple gallinule, a least bittern and some limpkins. These were the first of their species I'd seen since I started my life list a year earlier. With one hundred fifty-nine birds sighted and identified, I was still a novice birder.

Somewhere between Wakulla Springs and Crystal River I decided to spend a couple of days in Homosassa fishing from my skiff. Why not? It was the second week of May, when huge tarpon visit this stretch of Florida's Gulf Coast. Traveling Highway 98, I could reach Homosassa in about four hours, and I love the road. It's so unlike the interstate and turnpikes. It's the real Florida!

My journey through this sunshine state reminded me of those who had adventured before me: the many tribes of Seminole Indians, Spanish explorers with an unquenchable thirst to acquire territories, wealthy South Carolinians looking for escaped slaves, ocean-wise pirates and smugglers, sponge harvesters, recreational fisherman, commercial netters, and Cuban refugees from a Communist island. Oh, what a wonderful home this Florida makes. In a different time and place, I think I could easily have been a pirate, smuggler, sponge harvester, or even a commercial fisherman. It is the coastline of Florida that has always intrigued me. Even during our early vacations south, we always traveled by the coastal roads and highways. I read somewhere, or maybe it was the words of Imogene Taylor, my wise mother, that told me that Florida has the longest coastline of any state with the exception of Alaska. Florida's eight thousand four hundred miles of coastline, does not include the twenty-three thousand additional miles of shorelines along rivers and streams. All of this excites me and gives me an adventurous spirit eager to explore this extraordinary peninsula.

In the few years that I have taken up valuable space on this planet, I have been lucky enough to observe much of my home state's coastal areas such as: the sugar white dunes of Pensacola and Gulf Breeze with their sea oats swaying in the summer breezes; the grassy shores of the Gulf coast along the Big Bend area near Cedar Key with huge oyster mounds only inches away; Boca Grande and Captiva's ever-changing beaches of sand and shells inhabited with so many long-legged birds; the primitive Mosquito Coast between Chockoleskee and Everglades City, often referred to as the River of Grass; and of course my favorite, the Coral Rock Bottom that is habitat for the mangrove tree, many crustaceans and the elusive bonefish. This coral also provides foundation for the many bridges that make up the overseas highway, the very highway that will deliver me to my future home in the Keys. Perhaps one day I would have time to explore Florida's other coast, the Atlantic. But for now my mission was to get to Key West.

After stopping at about a dozen motels I realized May is indeed the tarpon season. "Sorry, no vacancies," was what I kept hearing. When I got the same reply at the Riverside Inn, I walked next door and talked to the guys at MacRae's Tackle. It was obvious they mostly sold bait and tackle to anglers in search of redfish and trout, but I still asked about tarpon and fly fishing.

Sitting in aluminum lawn chairs with most of the nylon webbing hanging to the floor, the crew from MacRae's was a colorful bunch. With the rapid increases in Florida's population, the towering cement condos running over sandy beaches and the huge chunks of Florida real estate being sold again and again, these guys had escaped it all. I was envious. These three native Floridians still lived in the Florida I loved. Unconsciously, I sized them up in my mind. The long, straight, greasy and dark-haired fella in the back was surely of Indian descent. The other silent body was of Greek ancestry. I pictured him and his family plucking sponges from the pristine ocean floor of Tarpon Springs, a few miles south of here. The one in charge, the one they called Mike, was more civilized. His short hair, absence of tattoos and pierced body parts, along with his big smile put me at ease. He was one of those replanted Georgia crackers that came to Florida to fish commercially.

The art of taking first impressions was a habit, good or bad as it may be, I had learned from my father. I sized these three up as if they were customers entering Taylor's Fine Jewelry Store. I would suggest opening a charge account for Mike. However, the other two would be on a cash-only basis. I felt rotten, evil even for thinking these thoughts. It was a hazard of the trade, one I needed to overcome. Mike gave me a few names of some captains in the area that specialize in catching tarpon on a fly.

"Most of them there guides have those little fancy saltwater bass boats and fish out of Tarpon Springs."

I looked around the counter to match a face with the voice. A head full of red hair with two stuffed cheeks of chaw, wearing a faded hat that read "Roll Tide," smiled back at me. I bought a Budweiser, thanked them and headed for my truck. On the back of my Dodge pickup was a sixteen-foot Maverick flats boat, a graduation gift from Charles Sr. and Imogene. Ever since I'd left Wakulla I'd been asked, "What's that thing over the motor?", "Is that to keep the rain and sun off your motor?", and "Is that a platform to hold your ice chest?" Now I was told it was a "saltwater bass boat." I threw the unopened bottle of Bud in the trash and decided to go to Tarpon Springs. Surely these guys had seen a picture of someone pushing a boat from a poling platform.

For me, standing on the poling platform above the engine, moving my skiff along the shore in water less than ten inches, is as much fun as the fishing itself. While standing on the platform, one's view is increased a thousandfold. Once a fish is spotted, the skill of advancing the skiff within casting range is indeed an art. It becomes a challenge, a hunt. At this point the fish has all of the advantages. The fish is easily alerted by factors such as shadows cast by the boat, noises from the fisherman, like loud voices, the slamming of ice chest lids or the shuffle of feet, wave action lapping the bow of the boat, and of course my favorite, A. E. This latter friend of fish is the hardest one for most fishermen to accept. For A. E. stands for "Angler Error."

"Nice boat you got there." I spun around expecting to see Sasquatch from the tackle shop again. It wasn't old fuzz face after all.

"Hi. I'm Captain Limbo," he said.

He was probably fifty years old, six foot two inches, weighed about 180 and was smiling from ear to ear. He reminded me of Sam Elliot. It was obvious he'd spent many an hour in the sun. He wore a hat with a long bill, dark sunglasses and his nose was white, covered with zinc oxide.

"Nice to meet you, Captain Limbo. I'm Powell Taylor."

Captain Limbo had a friendly way. After a couple of minutes I felt like we were best friends. The next thing I knew we launched the skiff and took off to the end of the Homosassa River to a little bar and grill called The Crow's Nest. Accessible only by boat it was a nice little out-of-the-way harbor.

The sun was soon to disappear for the evening as boats scurried past us in an effort to return home before the light fog rolled in over the river. The scent in the air was crisp and definite. It was a delightful mixture of humidity and salt mixed with the aroma of a cheeseburger grilling over an open fire at the pub.

"Hey, Limbo, we ought to get this place patented," I said.

He agreed.

It was a refuge, a retreat that should be open to public examination. But, it should also be protected by such a right, a process, a patent.

When we pushed up to the floating dock, cormorants stood proudly atop each piling. Their feathered necks turned as they watched our every move. Small alligator gars were rolling on the surface around us, sucking oxygen from the foggy nocturnal air. A huge school of bait peppered the surface of the river. The sprinkle on the water resembled a small rain shower. There was a piercing slurp in the center of the rain as a five-pound trout filled his mouth with more than a dozen minnows. This harbor brought me far away from Gulf Breeze Florida.

Captain Limbo looked as if he had spent many a night in pubs like this, so I was surprised when he ordered a nonalcoholic beer. I didn't ask; I ordered my Corona and lime and was a million miles from home.

The more we talked, the more I liked Limbo. After an hour or so I caught myself wondering if he earned his name from the island dance or his state of mind. Although he spoke slowly with a heavy southern accent, he was definitely not stupid. I learned that his real name was Dr. James Adams, who came complete with a doctorate in marine biology from the University of Alabama and a long list of published papers, articles, and a couple of books on marine life and conservation. One of his books, *Farming Shrimp for The Future* was used all over the south and was responsible for the shrimp aquaculture boom. I had the feeling that Dr. Limbo was far from destitute.

Before I knew it, my watch read eleven o'clock and the Crow's Nest was closing up. I told Captain Limbo I needed to get moving. I explained the motel situation and my trip south to the Keys.

"Hell, that's where I live, Powell. Why don't you stay here with me for a couple of days and fish? When we've had enough, we'll pack up and make the trip together." It was an offer I couldn't refuse.

Chapter Three

Captain Limbo had a comfortable cabin at MacRae's fish camp, complete with two double beds, microwave, air conditioning, a rack to hang your fishing rods and a marina complete with Big Foot.

More evidence of Limbo's apparently prosperous state peered across the parking lot as we approached my new abode. Attached to the rear of a rather new-looking four-wheel-drive vehicle was a shiny new Hewes light-tackle twenty-foot skiff. It looked like a picture out of one of those mail order catalogs for fly fishermen. "Even ol' Jacques P. Herter would have been proud to display this rig among the pages of his once popular outdoor catalogue," I giggled to myself.

The best I could figure from our conversations without prying too much, Dr. James Adams had gotten fed up with the politics of teaching in a state university. He resigned his position and moved to Hilton Head Island, South Carolina where Limbo spent five years in the seafood business. After a season of constant disagreements with the newly inherited management on questionable ethics and the means by which they obtained certain fish, Limbo severed himself from the business and vowed at that point to conserve and enjoy the waters. He would never again thieve them of sea life. When fly fishing, he would release every frustration along with each fish he hooked. This was not simply a flip decision: this was Limbo's philosophy, his religion, his new way of life. He even debarbed the hooks on his flies so they wouldn't harm the sensitive mouths of his prey. He handled his fish just long enough for their quick and safe revival. Limbo was practicing these self-taught morals long before they were in vogue within fly-fishing cliques.

On the rare occasions when Limbo might pick up a spinning rod to catch a snapper or grouper, he would only keep enough for one meal.

That evening, just as I was about to finally doze off in one of those double beds, I heard Limbo utter, "Get some sleep, Powell. We have a long day tomorrow." I didn't answer, hoping he would believe I was already sound asleep. Soon, I didn't have to fake it. The next thing I knew, I heard the cabin door open. I jumped out of bed and saw Limbo standing in the doorway soaking wet with sweat. It was four thirty a. m. and he'd just finished his daily six miles. I was still trying to focus on life when I heard him say, "Time to get moving Powell."

As Limbo showered, I rigged my tackle. My thoughts were back in Gulf Breeze: Charles Sr. and Imogene would still be asleep for another hour and a half. Then they would start their routine, preparing for another day of retail madness. I missed that routine already, but I forced those guilty and depressing thoughts from my mind. I rigged my 12- weight Sage fly rod with a Billy Pate tarpon reel spooled with about three hundred yards of backing, a 12- weight Mastery intermediate sink fly line and the prettiest tarpon fly I had in the box. I checked all of my knots and yanked on the 16 lb. tippet secured to the 12" of 100 lb. shock. Perfect. I splashed some water on my face to remove any of those little yellow crusty things that appear in the night and affix themselves to the inside of eyelids. I threw on some clothes and collected the necessary gear for the day: sunglasses, sunscreen, camera, binoculars, extra leaders and flies. I was ready to catch my first huge tarpon on a fly.

"Whose boat ya wanna take, Limbo?" I asked as he stepped back into the room.

"Neither one," he replied. "I chartered the best tarpon guide in the area for today. We'll fish on his boat. It's always a good idea to hire a guide when you fish a new area for the first time. You would be amazed at what all you can learn. Guides not only know the tides and moon phases and which tackle and fly to use, but also a good guide always knows where the fish live. It's definitely worth the cost of a charter to learn the area."

"Just how much is a charter?" I had to ask, knowing I didn't have an over abundance of cash with me.

"I'll get this today Powell, since I already had it booked anyway."

"Thanks!" I blurted, realizing a good guide cost more than I had to spend this week. As we pulled out on Highway 98, Limbo was telling me about our guide.

"His name is Ed Walker, he's twenty-five years old and knows more about tarpon than anyone on the planet."

"Sounds like exactly who we need to fish with," I said.

It was obvious that Ed had earned the respect of my new friend. As we drove, Limbo continued.

"Ed fishes for tarpon from early April through August every year. The remainder of the year he fishes for trout and redfish. In May and early June Ed fly fishes only in the Homosasassa area. Later, during June and July, he moves south to Boca Grande Pass. Ed's won quite a few tournaments over the years. However, the key to Ed's success is the fact that he loves tarpon and loves stalking them. He's the best tarpon guide I've ever seen."

I was so fascinated with Limbo's description I couldn't wait to meet and fish with Captain Ed Walker.

We turned right at Weeki Wachee Springs, heading west toward what I assumed would be the direction of the Gulf. After a few miles, Limbo pulled into a little diner called Becky's. I knew we were close to our destination. The parking lot was filled with an assortment of saltwater bass boats. Ed had just parked, and after spotting us he ran over to meet us at the door.

"Hello, Ed, how's it goin'?"

"Great, Limbo, long time no see."

"Ed Walker I'd like you to meet a new friend of mine, Powell Taylor."

After the introduction we sat down and ate a great country breakfast complete with eggs, grits and some link sausage that was sure to slow the blood flow through my arteries. Limbo had a bowl of grits and a tomato. As I was finishing off the last cholesterol bomb, I noticed all the local guides were trying to outdo each other's fish stories. What is it that is so appealing about telling untruths? I was always taught not to lie. Liars go directly to hell, do not pass purgatory, do not collect absolution. It always amused me. The different ways people handle lies. Fibs, little white lies, and stretching the truth are innocent definitions for liars. When a witness on the witness stand fabricates a story or tells lies, it's called perjury. When an attorney lies to the courts it's called legal representation. A writer uses the word fiction, or my favorite poetic license. Sister Consuella, my eleventh grade religion teacher, called it Mortal Sin. My mother would say lying is at the least a venial sin. But, to myself and these local fishermen, we were content to call it story telling. That's what most fishermen do, tell stories! Each guide had just a little better version than the other. I sat there in amazement as I listened to tales of tarpon jumping into boats, and about the pending world record fish caught yesterday on 12 lb. tippet.

It was obvious that the other guides respected Ed's fishing ability, in spite of his youth. They asked his advice and pressed for information that he willingly gave. At least I think he did. But then again, he may have been committing one venial sin right after another. We discussed tarpon fishing, women, tides, colleges, television and world politics in the very short time it took us to swallow breakfast. I was quite certain that Captain Walker was good at his profession. I also got the impression he didn't like outsiders coming from other areas to fish Homosasassa during peak season.

Knowing I was going to have a great day on the water with an excellent guide, I happily paid the tab. This charter would cost me $9.25. Limbo and I followed close behind Ed's rig to the boat ramp where he launched his 16' Silver King powered by a ninety-horse Yamaha. A bright new glossy blue color, Ed's skiff was the sharpest boat at the launch. I felt great as we powered out of the harbor and cleared the "No Wake" zone where we began to make good use of those ninety horses.

After a forty-minute run, Ed cut the motor and climbed atop the poling platform. I talked Limbo into taking the bow first. I wanted him to have the first shot at a tarpon, or at "Mr. Poon" as Ed called 'em.

The bow of the boat, where Limbo now stood, gives the angler a definite advantage. Although not as high in the air as the Captain on his platform, he is closer to the fish. Hopefully from this forward location, his straining eyes are able to see through the surface glare into the water to make out the silhouettes of the huge tarpon. It is very important to see the fish before you cast to them. Sometimes tarpon sit lifeless on the bottom making them near impossible to distinguish. Often they are slowly moving against the current. Other times they are swimming much faster. The best situation is when the tarpon swim in a circle on the surface. They remind me of the circus elephants. With their noses only inches from the tail of another fish, they follow and frolic with each other paying little attention to the presence of others. These fish are the happiest and easiest to spot. Still, it is important to see them before you cast. A short cast does not put the fly in the tarpon's view. Casting beyond the fish is even worse. As the fly line hits the water above the tarpon, he spooks and disappears as quickly as he appeared. You must see the fish in order to present the fly a few feet in front of the lead fish. By the time the fly sinks to their level hopefully it will enter the tarpon's view. This window is small, but being on the bow of the skiff brings you closer to success.

Limbo stripped out his fly line and made a couple of practice casts out to about seventy-five or eighty feet. He was a good caster, making the line zing through the guides with very little effort. The wind was 10 to 15 mph, out of the southwest. As a rule, beginning fly fishermen are most intimidated by the wind. I had learned over the years, as Limbo obviously had, to use the wind to your advantage. Don't ever let it get to you, don't let it grate on your nerves. Recovery is the name of the game. If you allow a bad cast or a bad presentation to bother you, it only gets worse. I saw a very good fisherman get so frustrated when he spooked several bonefish that he deliberately broke his four hundred dollar rod in half and threw the whole rig overboard. Now that's crazy. You're out there to relax and have a good time. Besides, if you relax, you'll cast a hell of a lot better.

Limbo would not have a problem with casting or with catching. "Tarpon! Ten o'clock, two hundred feet," yelled Ed.

I pictured in my mind a daisy chain of circus trained tarpon all five to six-foot long with their silver sides reflecting sunlight from saucer sized scales.

As I turned and tried to see the fish, Ed jumped down off the poling platform screaming and pointing.

"You god damn bunch of bean pickers, get the hell out of here and go back to New Jersey where you belong."

I spotted them the very moment Limbo did. A seventeen-foot Glastron boat painted bright yellow with a seventy-five-horse Chrysler engine crammed full of sunburned tourists. They were going full speed toward the school of fish Ed had spotted. Five feet from the tarpon the captain jerked back the throttle as the two men on the bow went head-first into the water. It was quite a sight to see as the two tourists, their tackle and dozens of beer cans sailed through the air.

Ed cranked his engine.

"I hope you fuckin' bean pickers drown," Ed bellowed as we sped past barely missing the bigger of the two swimmers.

After twenty minutes we stopped, and Ed hopped back up on the poling platform. While Limbo prepared for battle, he poled us parallel to the shore.

"There is some nervous water straight ahead at twelve o'clock about one hundred yards. Keep an eye on it," Captain Ed whispered.

Even with my polarized lenses, I was straining to see through the sun's bright glare on the surface of the rippled water.

"Here," Captain Limbo said while handing me a hat.

"Thanks, I forgot mine," I replied.

"Keep it, it's good luck."

I could sure use some good luck, not necessarily fishing luck but just in general, especially in the year ahead. Changing occupations, addresses and friends made good luck most welcome.

My new lucky cap was great-looking. It had a long leather bill, an adjustable strap in the back and a beautiful tarpon fly embroidered on the front. Above the fly were the words: "The Saltwater Angler, Key West Fla. "As Limbo was explaining that a friend of his owned the shop, Ed in a loud whisper said "Tarpon in range eleven o'clock."

He'd kept his eye on the fish, stalked them and positioned the boat perfectly so the school of tarpon was down wind at eleven o'clock, sixty feet from Limbo's rod. Captain Ed Walker was as good as his reputation claimed.

Limbo, with only one false cast, laid the fly two feet in front of the lead fish.

"Great shot, Limbo," I said as we three stared at the fly, waiting for it to disappear down the gullet of one of these huge silver giants.

With short five-inch strips, Limbo moved the fly right past the eyes of each tarpon in the school. The orange cockroach fly with its grizzly hackle was a perfect choice for these clear waters. Why then, did this perfectly throbbing bait imitation not entice one of these silver kings into eating? Limbo's discouraging scowl destroyed the mood as he retrieved the fly, foot by foot, all the way back to the boat. No takers. Why was this? The fly and its presentation were perfect.

"What's wrong with those fish," I asked, letting Limbo know I didn't suspect A. E.

The school swam right under us and seemed to pass for five minutes. Limbo picked up the fly and made an incredible back cast into the wind. A gorgeous cast, the fly slapped the water directly on the nose of a tarpon. In three seconds, one hundred of the prehistoric-looking fish disappeared.

"That's all right," Ed said, "Those fish were spooked. They weren't going to eat."

The next three or four hours passed quickly as Limbo and I took turns on the bow. We changed positions every hour. I had just five minutes of bow time left when I saw a tarpon roll at three o'clock. I pointed Ed in the direction and he immediately saw a silver flash. As he poled me toward the target, my knees were vibrating all the way up to my neck. I knew this would be my last chance of the day and possibly the best chance I would ever have.

I did not want this trip to end like all of my others: I'd never caught a tarpon on a fly. In fact, the only tarpon I'd ever caught was with Charles Sr. in Key West when I was fifteen. Although we always used spinning tackle, Charles Sr. and Jr. had some great times together.

There he was. Without thinking, I made one back cast and laid the fly directly in front of a pair of very nice "Poons." I felt the line get tight. I reared back and set the hook.

In that instant before the explosion of water, I was able to witness the most exciting sight of all my fishing days.

I could see a pulsating black and purple fly a foot below the rippled surface. Then, as if in slow motion, a huge silver head appeared just below the fly. With the fly an inch from the tip of his nose his eye rolled and was staring into mine. It was too late. He had already committed. He knew better than I what was next. Then, from this wall of water came the very leap that is responsible for so many being possessed by this beautiful animal. At the moment, I was unaware that these four seconds would deprive me of sleep for the rest of my stay in Homosassa.

The next fifty minutes of battle were unimportant. He would jump and I would bow. When his huge golden eye caught mine, he saw deep into my soul.

"What a beautiful creature," someone behind me exclaimed.

I was in a trance and did not hear any other conversation. The big fish made one last, tiring run before resting beside the gunwale of the skiff. "How 'bout a photo?" I said.

While pushing the fish forward and back forcing water over his gills, Ed replied, "I don't bring tarpon into the boat. It's not a good idea and it hurts the fish."

I pulled out the camera, handed it to Limbo with a few instructions, grabbed my rod and jumped overboard. This was the first tarpon I'd ever landed on a fly and I was going to have a photo. I positioned myself behind the tarpon being extra careful not to hurt him.

"Hurry up and smile so I can get a picture before the damn fish gets sun poisoning," Limbo said with a touch of sarcasm. That brought an instant smile. I heard the shutter click as the six-foot tarpon shook his head and disappeared into his camouflaged environment of grass and rock. His quick exit threw buckets of water on us all. We sat there for a moment with shit-eating grins on our faces.

This day had convinced me that I was on target with my future plans. I wanted to live the life of a guide and enjoy life in the Keys. I loved my new hat.

As we headed back to the ramp, I quizzed Ed on his profession.

"You've got it made, Ed. You fish every day, enjoy the outdoors and meet plenty of new people. You've got it made all right," I said like a sixteen-year-old kid who just got his first job.

"Yeah, you've got it made all right," Limbo chimed in. "Fishing every day in the sun from one hundred ten-degree heats to twenty-degree frosts. Most guides have some type of skin cancer by the time they're forty. You work every holiday and Sunday of the year. You have to buy a new outboard every year. You have no certain days off unless the weather is terrible or your customers cancel. If you're lucky, you fish two hundred days a year at three hundred and fifty dollars a day. That's seventy thousand dollars a year before insurance, medical bills, boat motor and trailer repairs, tackle, fuel, chum, flies, leaders, hooks, house payments, car payments, food, ice, beer, and oil, not to mention a little cash for dates. I say dates because most guides aren't married. If they marry, their wives usually leave because they'll never see you. And for the new and exciting people you meet, half of them are assholes from New Jersey who want to stand on the bow of the boat, cast only to eleven o'clock, forty feet off and expect the fish to eat the fly one hundred percent of the time in exact sync with the captain kissing his ass.

"What do ya think, Ed, has Powell got an accurate idea of life as a guide?" Ed smiled and commented, "It really ain't quite that bad."

"Hey, Limbo," I had to say, "you thinking about a career change or something?"

We all had a little chuckle as we helped pull the skiff out of the water and then headed back up Highway 98.

I felt good as I thought about my day, my friends and my fish. However, in all of the information and literature I've read about tarpon, they all had black eyes. Maybe it was a mutation or maybe it was a reflection of the sun, but this fish, my fish had a bright yellow eye the size and color of a key lime.

As I lay in bed that night, I was still certain I wanted to be a guide. All I could see was that eighteen-karat yellow eye still glaring my way.

Chapter Four ———

Day Two in Homosassa started early, again.

"You're wastin' time," Limbo yelled at six a.m. "We fishing today or what?"

"I'm not sure, Limbo, I figure I need to be in the Keys in a week and I was hoping to stop around Boca Grande for a couple of days. I also wanted to just look around Homosassa before I have to head south."

"I'll tell you what, Powell, let's fish today, go sight-seeing tomorrow and we'll leave the following day for Boca Grande. What'cha say?"

Although I was running a little low on cash, I agreed and hit the shower. I figured it was easier than an explanation or argument.

The water in the shower was just beginning to warm when Limbo beat on the door.

"I changed my mind. Let's go now. Hurry up! They're leav'n, uh, I mean I'll meet you down at the river. I'll have the boat loaded and ready. Get moving, step on it."

He caught me a little off guard with this sudden haste. I felt he was being a little mysterious. He started to say something and stopped, as if he'd caught himself divulging some deep, dark secret. And why were we launching in the river instead of going down to Weeki Wachee, like yesterday? "Maybe he's just nuts," I thought. "I mean I really don't know that much about him. Maybe he's some escaped murderer who seeks and destroys unwanted tourists. Could he be planning my disappearance up some hidden tributary of Homosassa River? Somewhere so desolate that my rodent eaten carcass would never be discovered."

"Get a grip," I thought. "Maybe I'm the one that's nuts."

I threw all my stuff in a bag, grabbed my rod and ran down to the marina. Limbo was standing there staring down the river and didn't see me until I jumped on the bow. The motor was already idling and we were moving slowly down-river in just seconds.

Limbo seemed very distracted, yet very focused. He peered ahead as if he were watching the boat ahead of us. In a no-wake zone, we were forced to creep along at about three miles per hour. Limbo looked impatient.

"What we going after today?" I said trying to break the ice.

"A biggun," he replied.

"Speaking of bigguns, that looks like Ol' Big Foot in that boat up ahead," I said.

"Where?"

"In that boat you keep staring at," I continued.

"I'm not staring and just how do you know him?" Limbo barked in a pissed off tone.

"I don't really know him, I just ran into him back at the tackle shop the day I arrived here. He's Big Foot, the asshole."

Limbo finally cracked a little smile and said, "You're right, he is an asshole, but his name is not Big Foot. People call him Lunker. He's supposed to be a great fisherman. Let's follow him a ways and maybe he'll lead us to a hot spot." Limbo could not possibly have thought I was that stupid. Something was definitely going on here and we weren't following Lunker to a fishing hole. However, I played along and agreed that we should follow. We stayed just out of sight of the boat. We followed his wake around bends, slowing and stopping occasionally to listen for his motor. We were bobbing and weaving through the estuaries until I didn't know north from south, or were they tributaries? I'm sure Limbo knew the difference. He seemed to know a little about everything, especially when it pertained to the outdoors. I only hoped he knew where in the hell we were and how to get out.

Limbo cut the motor and glided up into the saw grass. Lunker's wake had stopped and there was no engine noise. We could hear voices as we climbed out of the boat and sank down in muck to our knees. Limbo motioned with his finger at his lips to move along quietly. The closer we got, the louder the voices became. It was apparent that we were not approaching fishermen. A tremendous loud splash of water along with more voices let us know we were only a few feet from Big Foot. I crouched down behind Limbo to listen and I heard his camera click. "What the hell are you doing?" I whispered.

"I need pictures," he said.

"Of what?"

"Of them killing their supper," Limbo confided.

I looked over Limbo's head and could see what was happening. I felt sick. In the bottom of my stomach was a knot that sunk me further down into the mucky hole in the water. I knew I shouldn't make a sound, but I wanted to vomit. If I hurled my last meal, the sound would surely alert Lunker and his friends. He would probably remove the harpoon from the baby manatee and pierce my heart.

"I've got enough, let's get out of here," Limbo said.

We made it back to the boat and poled up river a bit before cranking the motor.

"I can't believe what I just saw. What kind of person would harpoon and gaff a baby manatee right out from under its mother?" I choked.

"A low life son of a bitch like Lunker used to," replied Limbo.

"Used to?"

"Yeah, I'm putting an end to his poaching days right now. These photos should do the trick."

We pulled over to the side of the river and Limbo plugged his cellular phone into the cigarette lighter. He punched in a number and began to talk. "Hello. We got him this time for sure. Send a boat to the far east end of Bittern Bayou near the big oyster mound.

You'll find 'em. " Limbo put down the phone and looked my way. "I guess I owe you an explanation Powell. I'll catch you up later. Right now I want to wait and see them arrest your 'Big Foot' and his friends."

I said that was fine with me; I still wasn't feeling too good.

Limbo was talking while watching in both directions. One direction for Lunker and the other for what I assumed would be the marine patrol.

"Powell, some of the old timers say manatee meat tastes a lot like pork. The Indians used to eat 'em back in the early days when Florida was not yet ruined by tourism, pollution, greed, overfishing and overpopulation. Nowadays there are just too damn many people, too many nets in the sea. Too many rats in this cage! Cages the size of Florida just don't have enough room for rats like Lunker."

I was now feeling a little better so I thought I'd join in the conversation. "Why don't the manatees hide or run when people come up to them?" I said.

"They're West Indian manatees and are an endangered species. They belong to an order of sea cows that include all the manatees and dugongs. They're also the only completely aquatic members that are herbivorous. In other words, Powell, they eat grass. "

I didn't want to sound stupid but I had to ask, "Why are they in here with all these boats? Like I asked before, why don't they run and hide?"

Limbo was definitely in his element. He transformed from Captain Limbo into Dr. James Adams, marine biologist. He then continued . . .

"These great mammals come in here for two reasons. One is to eat the vegetation that grows in the river. The other reason is that the water temperature in these rivers and springs is constant all year round. They move here in the winter months to avoid cold weather. The reason they don't run and hide, as you say, is simple. They don't know any better. You see, they have no natural enemies, except for man. In Florida they are strictly protected from hunters. That's why I'm helping catch Ol' Lunker and his boys. They're disgusting. However, the biggest problem in Florida is not from hunters. It's from boaters.

"You see, Powell, these West Indian manatees are slow-moving animals that graze while submerged for periods of up to fifteen minutes. They don't pay attention to the boaters and couldn't avoid them if they wanted to. Most manatees bear the scars of boat propellers and collisions with boats. Because there are so many people in this cage and because of the manatee's low reproductive rate, serious population declines due to habitat loss and accidental deaths seem very likely in the future."

"That's interesting, Limbo," I said. "I always just thought they were big cute animals everyone loved." I knew better than to ask more questions but I had to ask just one more.

"Limbo, you said something earlier about dugongs?"

"Yeah, dugongs, just like manatees, are sea cows.

"What's the difference?" I asked.

"Besides a few dental differences, dugongs lack nails on their flippers and their tails are notched, like a whale's. Manatees have nails on their flippers and their tails are not notched, but rather spoon-shaped. This is the difference between dugongidae and trichechidae. Florida has manatees."

My manatee lesson was suddenly halted when Big Foot's boat came roaring around the corner.

"Good," Limbo said. "They ought to run into a great little welcoming party real soon."

Before Limbo could finish his sentence, we heard sirens, and then saw the blue lights. I was surprised to see a solid black cigarette boat about thirty feet long with twin 225 outboard's and big white letters on the port side that read "CUSTOMS."

Lunker and his crew knew they were had. They just rolled their eyes and held their hands high.

Dr. Adams resurfaced as Captain Limbo once again. I was glad to see him back.

"Powell," he said, "let's head back to the room and pack. It's time to head south. Besides at dinner tonight I have a little explaining to do."

Limbo removed the film from his camera and threw it to the captain of the Customs boat as we idled by.

"Thanks, Doc," the uniformed man spit out as he grabbed the

film and placed it in a baggie. I felt relieved and comfortable, but also a little too involved as we cruised through the no wake zone back to the marina.

After cleaning up and packing our bags we decided to eat up the road at the Sugar Mill Bar and Grill. We were just early enough to miss the happy hour crowds. From a dimly lit corner booth, Limbo and I ordered a couple of huge Greek salads, a cup of coffee and a Corona. Limbo began his story.

"In Hilton Head I became involved with Customs when they were investigating the fishery I worked for. They knew after a little digging and probing that I was not involved in the illegal actions of the company. They began to ask questions and after a while relied on my stories. It didn't take long before I was so involved I couldn't wait to get evidence to put them away. You see, Powell, I despise a crook, especially one that makes money at the expense of our natural resources. Our environment is dear to me and when it's gone, all is lost.

"Anyway, back to the story. I started taking photos and getting every incriminating fact I could. I knew I would lose my job. But, I felt it was my responsibility to expose them for the insensitive, greedy crooks they were. To make a long story short, all my delving paid off. They indicted all of the owners and closed down the operation. I lost my job, of course. After a year-and-a-half of training, I now sometimes work with Customs on cases that interest me. I'm not exactly working for Customs, just with them. I'm kinda what you might call a modern day bounty hunter.

"If it's a worthy cause and I can make enough money to keep me going, I'll help out. For instance, in the case you witnessed today, I would have helped catch those creeps even if there wasn't a ten thousand-dollar reward."

"Ten thousand dollars?" I yelled. " Are you shitting me?"

Limbo smiled and handed me a piece of paper.

"Here, Powell, I appreciate the help today."

It was a check for two thousand dollars. Although it couldn't have come at a better time, I tried not to show it. I argued while attempting not to accept it just enough to convince myself and Limbo that I was serious. The real fact was, I wanted to jump up and down. I finally stopped the charade, thanked Limbo and told him how much it would help me out.

"Anyway, Powell, I'm done here in Homosassa and I have to get back to the Keys soon. I'm thinking about helping out with another little problem Customs has down in Key West."

Limbo offered to help me find a job in Key West until I could get my feet on the ground and start my guiding service.

"In fact," he said, "if I do decide to take the job in Key West I could use your help, Powell. All I can tell you is that it involves a big jewelry store in the Keys. You could make some really good money. Maybe enough to start your fishing business. When you get down there, give me a call and we'll study our options."

Limbo gave me his phone number and address on Summerland Key. "Sounds good, Limbo. But before I come down I think I'll visit Boca Grande Pass for a couple of days. I've heard how nice it is, and now that I have a little cash, well you know, it IS on the way."

The Sugar Mill door opened and a couple of long-haired, bearded fellahs with jeans and cowboy boots came in and began to unpack their guitars and fiddles. The band had arrived. My eye then got a glimpse of a long-legged, gorgeous brunette with a pair of the shortest white shorts I'd ever laid eyes on. Her perfectly rounded bottom and large chest were almost enough to keep me interested in staying for the music. But it was getting crowded and I had a long day of travel ahead. I'd have to catch this act another time.

Chapter Five ————

By eight o'clock a. m. I was on I-75 headed south once again. I would have about three-and-a-half hours of travel time to absorb the past week. Overall, I was happy with my life. I met a new friend and I was in control of my future for the first time ever. I wasn't sure what the future would bring, but it felt good to know I controlled my own destiny. What would Mom and Dad think about this week? "Maybe I'll give them a call when I get to Boca Grande," I thought. It's funny how your mind works when you get away and have too much time to think and meditate.

Gulf Breeze was not a bad place at all to call home, just a little confined for the moment. Was I homesick? Was I missing that life? No!

As I passed through Bradenton, I noticed a sign pointing east to "Lake Manatee State Park."A queasy feeling came over me immediately as I pictured that poor manatee on the bow of Lunker's boat as he was being butchered for groceries. Was I ready to face this sick world?

I pulled off 75 and headed south on 776 and finally arrived at Gasparilla Island. Boca Grande's home island connected to the mainland by a toll bridge. The toll was $3. 20 plus $1. 00 for each additional axle. I paid the four twenty and continued down the road. I was a little early for tarpon season and the island seemed somewhat deserted. By June first I was sure there wouldn't be room to walk.

I did notice a few Mercedes, Lexus, and Beamers parked around the manicured yards along the drive.

I pulled into a bank to cash my new check. I picked the prettiest teller of the bunch and immediately struck up a conversation.

"Hi, Dawn Landry," I said. Her name was on a name tag above the left pocket of her blue blazer.

"Hello," she replied.

"I'm new in town," I said as I searched her left hand and found no rings. "I was wondering if you know a good place I could stay for a couple of days. A place with a dock for my boat, and maybe a restaurant or two."

Dawn looked at my check, smiled and said, "Here, Mr. Taylor," as she handed me a Boca Grande visitor's guide. "For a good, clean, reasonable room, I'd suggest the Waterfront Motel. It's about a mile-and-a-half on your left. It's on Boca Grande Bayou, has docking facilities and a boat ramp."

"Sounds like just what I'm looking for. How about a restaurant?" I was thinking about just how I would charm her a little and then ask her to go to dinner when she said, "Most of the restaurants on the island are fancy and pricey."

Not exactly what I wanted to hear. "Now what," I thought.

"However, Mr. Taylor . . ."

I interrupted, "Every time you say Mr. Taylor I turn to see if my father followed me down here. My name is Powell."

She laughed and said, "OK, Powell, there is a great little restaurant called Barnacle Bill's about twenty minutes from here, over in Englewood."

We both started talking at the same time, neither of us hearing a word the other had uttered.

"Excuse me, please go ahead," I said.

I was in a trance as I gazed at her beauty. Dawn had beautiful blonde hair, big bright blue eyes, a gorgeous smile and the body of an aerobics teacher. She was probably five-foot five and weighed about one hundred and ten pounds. I guessed her to be twenty-five or twenty-six years old. An older woman with huge tits. I mean breasts. Tits is too harsh a word for such a goddess, I thought.

"Well, what 'cha think, Powell?" she said.

I hadn't heard a word she had said the whole time. I was too busy gawking between the top two buttons on the blazer.

"Powell, are you listening to me, or are you too busy staring at my tits?" I could have crawled under the desk.

"I'm sorry, Dawn, but you are very pretty and I was not listening because I was trying to come up with a line to ask you out. I'm sorry."

"Don't be sorry, Powell. If you'd listened, you'd know that I just asked you to take me to Barnacle Bill's tonight. I get off at five fifteen."

"Great!" I said just a little too loud. "I'll go unpack, get settled in the hotel and launch my boat. I'll have just enough time to clean up and meet you back here at five fifteen. Sounds perfect!"

"I look forward to it Powell, and thanks for making me feel special today."

After passing eleventh street twice, I finally circled around and found the Waterfront Motel. It's not that it was difficult to find. My mind was on a temporary leave of absence.

The motel had a quaint, homey atmosphere with a relaxed and casual charm. It was ideal, right down to the barbecue grills on the back porch overlooking the canal. I checked in at the lobby with a nice lady who told me all about the place.

"The pool is always open, the boat launch is on the other end of the motel and we have fresh coffee and Danish every morning at 7:00 a. m. There's bike rentals across the street and we have a bike path that runs the entire length of the island. The railroad pulled up their old rails that led to the phosphate docks and paved them for bike trails."

"Great! I really appreciate all the info," I said while stepping over the lady's pet boxer as I left. The dog never even opened his eyes. Had I not noticed his chest cavity moving, I might have thought he was stuffed by the same taxidermist that furnished the tarpon and snook hanging on the walls. I made my way back to room B-10 and popped open a cold Corona. I cut a slice of lime that was just a little too big to force down the neck of the bottle. I finally managed it. I sat on the porch, looking at the peaceful scene of pelicans, mangroves and my skiff. Thinking of those poor fish that gave their lives to decorate the lobby walls brought my day dreams back to my youth. Once again I was back in Gulf Breeze.

As a junior in high school I decided I could make a fortune in taxidermy. I filled out the coupon in the back of my *Outdoor Life* magazine and sent it in with most of my savings. The Northwest School of Taxidermy along with Jaques P. Herter's book on taxidermy would educate me on my new career: stuffing animals and fish.

That was one more of my hair-brained schemes and hobbies that Charles Sr. and Imogene encouraged. Although Mom and Dad never said "I told you so," I sure wish I had part of the money back I'd spent on those great ideas. Between the surf boards, skate boards, guns, tents, sleeping bags, sailboats, cars, canoes, taxidermy, tackle, outboards and all the "stuff" that goes with it, I could have bought Boca Grande.

My parents always went along with my crazy ideas. Charles Sr. even helped me in my taxidermy venture. After I completed all my lessons from the Northwest School of taxidermy and passed my final exams I was ready to make my fortune.

The first animal I mounted for profit was a beautiful fox squirrel. When I finished him, I was so proud, I talked the owner into letting me keep him. When he came to pick up his squirrel, it was obvious that he had been drinking. After begging and pleading with the owner I offered him twenty dollars. He agreed.

So after lessons, chemicals, supplies, books, glass eyes, body material, tools and my first big job, I was about three thousand dollars in the hole. I'd make it up later, I figured.

My second attempt to stuff for profit was even better. The word was out. Powell Taylor had graduated Taxidermy 101. One afternoon my mother told me to call one of our neighbors.

"Powell, I've got a possum for you to mount," he said.

"Great! Mr. Bell, I'll be right down."

I ran as fast as I could. I took a garbage bag to put him in. That way, if Mr. Bell had shot him, the blood wouldn't leak out and I could just throw him in Mom's freezer. Lesson # eight: freeze small animals and as they thaw they'll become much easier to skin.

As the front door opened, I heard a hissing sound coming from the croaker sack Mr. Bell held.

"Hello, Powell, I caught this fellah in my garden. I knew you were doing taxidermy and thought you would like him. I caught him in a Have-a-Hart trap. Good luck!"

I had to search deep for a reply. "Oh, thanks a lot Mr. Bell, I really appreciate him."

I didn't know the damn thing was going to be breathing. Now what? I took him home, trying to decide the best method to end ol' "Pete's" life. I named him on the way home.

I didn't want to shoot him, for a couple of reasons. One, the mess it would cause, and secondly, I didn't want to repair the hole in his hide a bullet would make. From my high school days, I remembered that possums, or rather opossums, are one of the two strange animals that are native to American soil. The other is the armadillo.

The opossum has been a source of interest and wonder since the 1500s. It was Captain John Smith who wrote in English the first description of the "Virginia" opossum and bestowed upon it the Indian name, opossum, by which it is still known.

Opossums are marsupials, or pouched animals. Although in prehistoric days they roamed every continent, today they are only found in the Americas, Australia, Tasmania and a few islands to the north. I snapped conscious for a moment, smiling as I remembered why I knew so much about this disgusting animal.

When I was a junior in high school, the "in" word was "possum." The good words had already run their course. Words like bitchin' and radical were obsolete now. Everybody was "possum." One day in religion class Sister Mary Consuella asked me some deep questions on Theology. I said "Sure, possum. I know that." It just kind of slipped out.

The poor ol' nun just about stroked out right there. We never really knew how old she was, but the rumor was she served the Last Supper.

By the time I wrote opossum on the black board one thousand

times and wrote a twenty-page essay on opossums, I knew not only how to spell their name but everything else about them. The most important lesson I learned was not to call anyone that wore a habit, possum.

I had always heard that drowning was a peaceful way to die. I also remembered that opossums play dead and go into a state of death-feigning hibernation when faced with danger. I wanted to be as humane as possible. I at least rationalized that I was being humane. I got a large brick, put it in the sack with ol' Pete and threw him off the end of the dock for a couple of hours. He would just go into a peaceful sleep and never wake up. It didn't exactly go as planned.

After two hours under water I retrieved the croaker sack to begin skinning. I took my scalpel and began an incision down Pete's belly. When I poked him with the knife, he jumped up and bit the shit out of me. He then started hissing like a tea kettle. I tied up that sack and threw his hairy ass overboard one more time. There was more to this "playing possum" than I realized. I returned the next morning, poking and jabbing his hide to make sure I had no more surprises. Pete had passed.

When the incision revealed the lower half of Pete's abdomen, I suddenly realized this was not a Pete. It was a female with a pouch full of small embryo possums still connected to an umbilical cord. I got sick to my stomach and very light headed. I was about to throw her pitiful hide overboard when Charles Sr. showed up. He convinced me that if I did, indeed, discard Miss Pete, she and all her pups would have died for no reason. I somehow completed the task and Miss Pete has stayed alive over the years as a model in the window of Dad's jewelry store. His window dresser keeps the possum current on fashion. One month she'll wear diamond earrings and pearls. On Christmas she's Santa-Possum. Miss Pete's been everything from Easter Possum to a Mardi Gras party animal. One thing for sure: she's always been the center of conversation.

Pete was the last animal I would ever kill in my life. I swapped all my guns for fly reels and tackle. My taxidermy career had ended and my days of killing were over. I wouldn't miss it —ever!

Reality returned. I jumped out of bed and ran over to the table to hunt for my watch. It was four forty-five. Just enough time to shower and shave and get to the bank by five fifteen. I arrived a few minutes early. The bank closed at five o'clock so all doors were locked. I decided to wait outside in the parking lot standing near the passenger's side of the car. This way, I wouldn't feel awkward about walking around and opening the door for Dawn. I would already be within reach of the door handle. I'd just nonchalantly lean over, lift the handle, and help her into the seat. "Mr. Smooth," I thought.

At precisely five fifteen the back door opened and there she was. Dawn Landry had changed clothes and I was even more amazed with her looks. She had a natural beauty like no other girl I had ever seen. She wore white shorts with a white halter top and a lightweight linen jacket. With her tan she looked like she just stepped off the cover of *Glamour* magazine.

Mr. Smooth said "Hello, gorgeous" as I leaned over, gripped the car door and just about ripped my fingernails right out of their cuticles. The door was locked.

It was a twenty-five minute drive to Englewood. Dawn talked the whole twenty-five minutes without stopping. I was glad she was so outspoken and talkative. It made it easy on me.

We hit it off better than expected. I felt very comfortable with Dawn's company by the time we arrived at Barnacle Bill's Tavern. Englewood seemed to have a more casual attitude than its neighbor, Boca Grande. The parking lot of Barnacle Bill's was packed with cars from all over the states. The streets were crawling with tourists and all the little shops were teeming with customers. I saw every type of boat made being pulled to and from the direction of the ocean. It reminded me of the island Amity, in the Jaws movie. This place was alive.

Barnacle Bill's was a rustic wooden building with a long bar, loud music, hanging nets, stuffed trophies and neon signs. I liked Dawn's choice for our first date. We ordered a couple of soft-shell crab po-boys and a pitcher of cold draft. The more we drank, the better we knew each other. Dawn told me all about her past life while I told her all about my plans for the future. She seemed interested in my decision to guide and live in the Keys. She said that she always wanted to visit Key West but never quite made it. I described everything I could remember about the southernmost city and she said that one day she would come visit me and I could take her fishing. I agreed it would be a date to look forward to.

After the fourth pitcher of beer we knew all there was to know about one another. We sat there joking with each other till they closed the place down. Ours was the only vehicle left in the parking lot.

I remember kissing her good night at the bank and following her home to make sure she arrived safely. However, I don't remember finding my way back to my room at the Waterfront Motel.

The phone woke me at seven-thirty the next morning. I sat up trying to remember what day of the week it was. I remembered, hoping the call was from Dawn, because I forgot to get her telephone number at home. I knew everything about the girl except her telephone number. I was also quite sure I'd never find my way back to her house. It all seemed a little fuzzy at the moment.

"Hey, Powell, get your lazy ass out of bed. The day's a wastin' away."

Although I was really happy to hear from him, I had to mutter, "Hey, Limbo, not so loud, I can hear ya just fine."

"What's the matter Powell? A little too much partying last night?"

"Something like that," I replied. I told him all about my newest friend, Dawn, and how we had really gotten along so well. He was happy for me he said and then asked when I was going to be in the Keys. I told him I wasn't really sure. "What day is it anyway? I asked.

"Saturday!" he said.

"I guess I'll stay the weekend and leave sometime Monday. I'll be in the Keys Monday evening. Why do you ask, Limbo?"

"I may have that job for you in a jewelry store down here. It'll just be for a couple of months, till you save up some money to start your guiding.

"I'm working on another case and could use a little inside help. I'll explain more about it later if you're interested."

"Yeah, I'm interested, Limbo. I'll talk to you Monday evening about it." I got directions to his house along with his phone number before we hung up.

Next, I picked up the phone book and looked under the Ls. No Dawn Landry, no D. Landry, not even any Landrys. Great, it's Saturday, the bank is closed and I don't know how to find the best-looking girl on the island. I laid back down on the bed. My head was still spinning slightly. I must have dozed off again, because when the phone rang again, it was ten-thirty.

"Do you feel as bad as I do, Powell?" said the voice from the other end.

"Worse, I think."

"What are you doing, Powell?"

"Just laying here in bed, watching the ceiling pattern above and thinking about you."

"That's funny" she said. "That's the same thing I'm doing."

We told each other what a great time we had and how we really enjoyed each other's company. She thanked me for being a gentleman and for seeing her home last night. I couldn't help but to think, that had I not been quite so drunk, I wouldn't have been quite the gentleman I appeared to be.

"Look, Dawn. I have to leave Monday morning for the Keys. I was wondering if you would like to do something this weekend before I go."

"Sure, Powell, I'd love to! I've got a great idea," she said. "There's a little island south of here called Cayo Costa with no roads or bridges. The only access is by boat. Let's go over this afternoon and spend the night camping out on the beach. It's pretty remote and we can fish and picnic and probably never see another person."

For a minute I thought I must have been dreaming.

"I'll fix us a picnic basket," she continued. "You get your boat and tackle ready and I'll come by the motel about two-thirty this afternoon."

"That sounds great, Dawn, I'll have everything ready when you get here. I'm in room B-10."

"See you then, bye-bye."

I fueled the skiff, loaded the ice chest with beer, wine, fruit and ice. I was waiting on the dock when Dawn arrived at exactly two-thirty. She was stunning even without makeup. She leaned over and gave me a little kiss on the cheek as she boarded my Maverick. "I could love this girl in no time," I thought. After a twenty-minute ride from Boca Grande Pass, Dawn pointed out a place on the island to pull in. It was a peaceful sandy beach in the middle of nowhere. We beached the boat and hauled all of our gear up and made a little camp. We put out some blankets and positioned the ice chest and food nearby.

"I'm going to slip into my swimsuit and take a swim, Powell."

"That sounds like a good idea. Let's take a swim," I said.

Dawn went behind the bushes and in a couple of minutes returned wearing the bottoms only of a tiny bikini. She was not shy about showing her breasts. Of course I couldn't blame her. They were the finest pair I'd ever seen. She could have posed for any magazine in the country.

"Let's go, Powell," she said as I stood there with my mouth gaping wide open. The Gulf water was crystal clear and dead calm, not a breath of wind anywhere. We swam out about thirty feet till the water was chest high. I dove underwater and came up inches from Dawn's face. We gazed into each other's eyes for about ten seconds. I leaned over and gently kissed her lips. She smiled and kissed me back. We were the only two people on earth for this breathtaking moment. My heart was pounding loudly as she pressed her breasts against my chest. Her nipples were so hard I was aware of their constant pressure against me. She ran one hand slowly down my arm and took my hand and placed it under her left breast. As I massaged her, she reached down with her other hand and removed the bottom of her swim suit. I then began to kiss her down her neck until I reached her nipples. I kissed them one at a time, alternating between the two. I licked and kissed her up and down. She was moaning in ecstasy. She gently reached down with both hands, unzipped my shorts and removed my clothes. We were two naked bodies so in tune with each other, nothing else mattered. A boat went by and we both ignored it. I picked her up and walked back to the beach. I laid her down in six inches of water only a few feet from shore. She spread her muscular thighs, reached up and with her hand placed me in her. I plunged forward as she screamed with excitement. We rolled around in the surf for an hour, taking turns controlling each other's fantasy.

Afterwards we just laid in the water holding one another, talking and enjoying the moment. We watched the sun set before returning to camp. We started a fire, ate our supper and sipped wine. Dawn finally dozed off with her head on my shoulder slightly after midnight. I admired her striking form under the moonlight. She was still naked from earlier in the afternoon when we had shared the most intimate moment of my life. It would be hard to leave such a vivacious lady behind, come Monday. I closed my eyes and for the first time since my departure, thought of things other than my family.

The sun was up early. It would be another calm, hot day with no breeze. We walked the beach hand-in-hand talking and sharing grins.

After noticing quite a few snook cruising the beach, I ran back to camp and grabbed my rod. I threw about three different flies at the passing fish before I found a winner. I tied on green and white clouser. The minnow imitation with its white bucktail belly, green bucktail dorsal, flashabow sides and lead eyes thrown a couple feet in front of the fishes nose worked every time. It was a shame this day would have to end. It was like being stranded on a deserted island with a gorgeous woman. All there was to do was to fish and make love. I had certainly done my share of both on this last day in Boca Grande.

As we crossed the channel headed back to the motel, things got quiet. Neither of us wanted this to end. Thinking thoughts that I would never see Dawn Landry again saddened me. I think she was having similar thoughts.

"When you coming back to see me, Powell?" she whispered in a soft voice.

"Right after you come visit me in the Keys," I replied.

We both agreed that as soon as I got settled into a place in the Keys, she would come visit. Although I didn't really believe it would ever happen, it sounded good for the moment.

She helped me put the skiff back on the trailer and get my stuff packed so I would be ready to head out early the next morning. Our goodbyes took an hour and a half. We finished our farewell in the shower. The Waterfront's hot water heater ran out after about twenty minutes. Dawn's blue eyes were watery as she drove off that evening.

The next morning, I grabbed a couple of muffins and a cup of coffee in the lobby as I checked out. I was on the road by seven-fifteen, headed for my future paradise. I was sad as I passed the bank on my way out of town. Dawn was probably just beginning to wake and face the new week.

Although I was in a hurry to reach Summerland Key and meet up with Limbo, I decided to take the more scenic route. I continued south on highway 41 and cut across Florida on the Tamiami Trail. It was a deserted stretch with an overabundance of air boats and Indians. Former trading posts were now souvenir shops and convenience stores. I had the distinct feeling that I was an outsider in a world that did not include me. Air boat rides seemed to be the largest source of income for the dark-skinned Seminole Indians along this fifty-mile stretch across the Florida Everglades.

I felt a little relieved as I reentered the 20th century at Florida City. "The Gateway to the Florida Keys," the sign read. I was on familiar ground as I left highway 41 and joined US 1: a magnificent highway that starts in Maine and ends in Key West. I remembered that on every trip our family made to Key West we stopped for photos at the Southernmost Point, Mallory Square and the Key West Court House. The Court House was the site of a large sign constructed at mile marker zero that said, "End of the Rainbow." For our family it brought much more pleasure than a pot of gold.

I stopped in Key Largo, the first key in the chain of islands and the first of the hundreds of bridges that link the Florida Straits.

I stopped for fuel, a bite to eat, and a phone call.

"Hello, Powell? Where are you? How have you been? We miss you something terrible, " cried Mom's voice from the other end of the phone.

"I'm fine, Mom. I'm just now getting to the Keys. I met a guy that lives on Summerland Key who said I could stay with him until I find a place of my own. He's a great guy and is going to help me get a job in a jewelry store in Key West."

"A jewelry store? I thought you were going to fish for a living or something?"

"Yes ma'am, I'm going to guide, but until I get settled and am able to build up some clients, I'll need an income. Captain Limbo, that's his name, is going to help me. I think he knows the owner of the jewelry store. He also guides and fishes for a living."

I surely didn't tell her Captain Limbo worked for Customs and that my job might be connected somehow.

"OK, Powell, when you get somewhere with a phone, call and let us know your number. Here's your dad, love you."

"I love you too, Mom, I'll keep in touch."

"How's it going, Son?"

"Great, Dad. I miss all ya'll up there though. Things seem to be falling into place here after all. I was telling Mom I might work in a jewelry store in Key West for a while, just till I build up my charters."

"Powell, if you decide to stay in jewelry you know you are always welcome and we always have a place for you here at the store. It would be a good living."

"I know, Dad, and I really appreciate it, but I want to give this a try. It's been my dream ever since the first time you dragged us down here on vacation. "

"Those were some fun times, weren't they, Powell?"

"Yes, sir, and as soon as I have a place of my own, I want ya'll to pack up and come visit. I'll take you fishing."

"That's a good plan, Powell. I'll look forward to it. I'd let you talk to your brother, but he's gone to the beach. This is the weekend MTV hosts the volleyball championships. He said he's interested in the game. I say he's interested in those girls' swimsuits or, rather, lack of them. Drop us a line when you get settled."

"OK, Dad, and tell Brad I said hello. Miss ya'll. Bye bye."

"Good bye, Son," he said as he hung up the receiver. I was saddened for a few moments; I wondered why I never found it easy to tell my father that I loved him. He had never told me that he loved me, either. I did indeed love him and I was sure he loved me. It was a pity that we couldn't easily tell each other how we felt. When and if I ever have kids, that will be a priority, I told myself as I pulled back out onto U.S. 1.

I noticed the little green rectangular sign on the side of the road that read 99. I was at mile marker number 99. I love these little signs. In the very relaxed and reckless attitude of living the "Keys Disease" life, you're never lost. It is impossible to go an entire day without hearing the words "mile marker." All directions and landmarks are only given by mile markers.

"You have to try this little pub and sandwich shop. Turn right at mm 35."

"I caught the biggest tarpon I ever saw, under the bridge at mm 52."

"We have six different locations throughout the Keys, mm 100, 79, 53, . . ." etc., etc., etc.

I just love the uniqueness and the simplicity of mile marker signs.

One day soon I would come back up to Key Largo and spend a couple of weeks making the 100-mile journey to Key West. I'd start at mm 92 to snorkel Pennecamp Coral Reef. From there I'd take my time and visit every interesting place along the way. Tackle shops, dive shops, restaurants, bars, marinas, national parks, glass bottom boats, dolphin shows, none would escape my extensive tour. But, for now I was in a hurry to get to my destination, mm 28: Summerland Key.

I passed over the hundreds of low lying tropical isles paying special attention to this place. There is no mystery as to why people visit the Keys. This Florida is different from the Florida I visited yesterday and the day before. Great white herons flock to their rookeries among the red mangrove thickets. Osprey and their young sit in nests atop obsolete telephone poles along U. S. 1. With one eye they scan the ocean for a meal, the other eye watching as a thousand tourists pass daily beneath them. In the shallows near the highway, the sun reflects on the flats as long legged ibis and egrets search the grass and coral for anything edible. Standing only a few feet from the speeding cars, campers and greyhound busses these assorted wading birds seem a bit too tame. A splash in a nearby channel catches my eye. I see a fluorescent orange snorkel disappear as two black flippers surface. A strong kick sends the diver to the bottom. A red flag tied to the swimmer bounces up and down in the water to announce the diver's presence as he scans the coral floor for colorful tropical fish, sponges, sea fans and lobster. My eye moves to a sight not so attractive. On the northern side of the highway, the Gulf side, a strip shopping center is being built on a narrow piece of land among the mangrove trees. It looks hideous and pisses me off. How can such beauty coexist with such shame?

I found his house with no problems at all. Captain Limbo was out back on his dock overlooking a canal giving one of his neighbors fly-casting lessons.

"I finally made it, Limbo," I yelled out.

"Good to see you, Powell," Limbo said before introducing me to his neighbor.

We cast a while, and talked about my trip. After the neighbor left, I unpacked and moved into Limbo's guest room. From the looks of Captain Limbo's house, it could be said that he was a true scavenger. Anything that floated up on shore was either nailed to his house or dock. I guess he should be admired for his closeness to nature and his back-to-the basics sort of life. But catching rainwater and storing it in large cisterns, waiting for the sun to heat the water so you can shower, is not my idea of comfort. I need a shower with running hot and cold water, one luxury I feel I cannot do without.

Thoughts come to mind about all the people back in the cities bitching about their power bills. I suddenly had the power company's solution. They should give all of these unhappy people a few weeks vacation at Capt'n Limbo's. Not only would they quit their complaining, they'd think electricity was damn cheap. The only positive side of no electricity is, you never have to watch the Cosby show spin-offs.

"After your interview tomorrow with Caribbean Jewelers, I thought I'd take you fishing," Limbo said. "About thirty miles west of Key West is the very place that will help you realize why you want to be a flats' guide. It'll take your breath away. The horseshoe- shaped mangrove islands that make up this atoll called the Marquesas will haunt you the rest of your life. The vision of the pristine flats you'll witness will stay in your mind like the memory of the first beautiful lady you ever loved. It will be with you forever. You'll never be able to get enough."

As Limbo left the room, I wondered how any place could fill my mind like the vision that occupied most of my skull lately. The Marquesas would have to invite some divine power to help squeeze Dawn Landry from my thoughts. Limbo returned with some Key Lime pie and Cuban coffee. The pie was tasty and the con leche strong. He said he copied the recipe for the pie off of a post card he picked up in Islamorada. Limbo was an unusual person.

I slipped away too quickly that evening. Dawn and I didn't make it out to the Marquesas before I fell off into a deep sleep.

Chapter Six ────

The sound of my fingernails tapping on the oak desk brought me out of a trance as I stared down at the application. I looked at my wrist, gazing at the word Seiko on the dial. "Damn," I thought. I had been daydreaming for eleven minutes. In twenty-three and a half years, this was my very first job application to fill out.

I found myself wondering just what in this manicured setting of the rich and famous could Customs be so interested in; interested enough to have Limbo spying on them. Was I to be an accessory to Limbo's paranoia or did I just want a job? For now, I would be happy with merely knowing I would have some sort of income. I needed enough money to get out from under Limbo's (metal) roof. I needed AC, hot showers and a daily routine. Although I was deeply in debt to Limbo for his gracious hospitality, it would not be a sad departure when the day came. The money I had saved over the years would be put to good use. It would be the way to my new abode. But, without a job I could not comfortably move out. After all, the Keys are not the cheapest places in the U. S. to live.

I read over the application one more time. Everything seemed to be in order. I used my Gulf Breeze address to avoid connecting myself with Limbo. This should satisfy Customs and hopefully I would make my split from Bedrock soon.

My application looked impressive for someone who was only twenty-three years old and just out of school. Graduate gemologist and diamond appraiser from the Gemological Institute of America (GIA), a jeweler with eight years experience at the bench, engraver, gift wrapper, salesman, appraiser, polisher, floor sweeper, and computer operator. I felt as if I was qualified to work for Mr. Winston Sloan and would be an asset to the Caribbean Jewelry Co. of Key West, FL. In fact, that was exactly the last thing I wrote on the application.

"Are you finished, Mr. Taylor?" I turned to see that her face was as attractive as her voice. She was a tall, thin brunette with big brown eyes and a friendly smile.

"Yes, ma'am," I replied.

"Good! I'm Jennifer Allen and I'll give you a little tour and some history of our store. I'll also fill you in on all the gossip I know."

Jennifer looked to be a couple of years younger than me and appeared to genuinely love her job. She was enthusiastic, friendly and kept a big smile on her face at all times.

"On the front floor we usually have three sales people, Mr. Sloan, myself and hopefully you, Mr. Taylor. That would complete our sales staff.

"Please, Jennifer, call me Powell," I said, trying to muster as much excitement in my voice as possible. I wanted to be part of this team, and I had a feeling Jennifer had a fair amount of pull with Mr. Sloan. I needed to impress her.

"Well then, Powell, we have four full-time jewelers, an engraver, two bookkeepers, one receptionist, one typist and computer operator, two watchmakers, and a part-time window dresser." Jennifer explained. "We also have a cleaning crew that comes in each evening. We normally employ about sixteen to eighteen people, including Mr. Sloan."

"How long have you worked here, Jennifer?" I said.

"Since I was eighteen, about three years," she replied. "I kinda keep an eye on things when Mr. Sloan is away. He trusts me and in return I really work hard for him."

"Do you do the hiring?" I asked.

"No, Mr. Sloan does all the hiring and firing. But from the looks of your application I don't think you have anything to worry about. Besides, you already have my vote."

"Thanks, Jennifer, I appreciate that. You're very kind."

I could tell from glancing into the showcases that Caribbean Jewelry Co. carried a high end of fine jewelry. Fourteen and eighteen karat gold high-fashion bracelets and chains gleamed from one case. The first case on the left as you entered the store was brimming with diamond and colored stone jewelry. I did notice that the emeralds were also very high quality. The next case beautifully displayed Mikimoto pearls and jewelry. The fine quality pearl strands, bracelets, earrings and rings were almost identical to the Mikimoto display Charles Sr. had back in Gulf Breeze. Various expensive lines of Swiss watches filled the wall cases. Mixed in were plenty of Seikos. I wondered for a moment who the salesman for South Florida was. Certainly not ol'—naw, couldn't be. Wrong coast! Jennifer hurried me past the other cases to show me the back of the store where the jewelers were working. They were in a room all to themselves. Four benches lined up with a polishing motor, steam cleaners, and plating machines. It was very similar to Taylor's Jewelers in Gulf Breeze with a couple of exceptions.

Charles Sr. always insisted that customers want to see who works on their jewelry. He always had the jewelers in full view of the sales floor. He said, "Nobody wants you to put their precious jewelry in an envelope and then run off into a back room." I agreed with him on that particular part of business. Sometimes the ladies would watch as we set their diamonds or sized their rings. Everyone felt more comfortable, but it was obvious that Mr. Sloan did not share our thoughts on this idea.

The other difference was that Caribbean Jewelers had spotlessly clean and organized benches. Dad's benches were total chaos. The jewelers never had time to clean them. They were too busy working on special orders, stock jewelry or daily repairs. The benches at Taylor's got cleaned up twice a year. That was New Year's Eve and the Saturday before our annual two-week vacation in July. There was always something that had to be rushed. Customers were always leaving town tomorrow or getting married Saturday, graduating soon or getting engaged as soon as the ring was ready.

I always thought that these two differences are what made Charles Sr. so successful. He did whatever it took to make his customers happy and would always do it as soon as possible. That and the fact that he is the most honest man I ever knew were the reasons for his much earned success. Besides, he worked his ass off his whole life.

"Maybe when and if I got this job I'd make a few recommendations to Mr. Sloan. I better just be happy to get work," I thought.

"What's behind that door, Jennifer?" I said.

"That's the security office. We're not allowed in there, Powell. It's set up with cameras, alarms and vaults for the entire store."

After reading his name on the door I had to ask, "Who's Harrison Gray?"

"He's the head of security, but I've only seen him a couple of times. He works mostly in the evenings after the store closes."

That was just a bit strange, I thought. Gulf Breeze must be really lucky not to have enough severe crime to warrant the need for a full-time security office in its retail jewelry stores.

"I wouldn't think that Key West would have that much crime."

"Don't worry, Powell, we've only had a couple of problems and they were minor, after-hours incidents. No one has ever been hurt.

"Well, that's enough about that. We have all the information we need for now. We'll check your references out and get back with you. This phone number, is it in the lower Keys?"

"Yes," I replied. "It's up on Sugarloaf Key. I'm staying with a fishing guide up there for a few days."

After I thanked them for the opportunity to apply, I thought I'd walk around Key West a while.

Duval Street had changed slightly since my last visit.

A mile long, Duval stretches from the Gulf of Mexico to the southern most house on the Atlantic ocean. Duval Street in its whorish splendor is delicately balanced between vulgarity and grandeur. Next door to a fine art museum is a store window display of lewd underwear and an assortment of leather paraphernalia for men.

This street that was named before Florida even became a state has it all. Besides the tourist shops, bars and taverns, art galleries, fine restaurants, dive shops, tackle and clothing stores, jewelry companies, and post card outlets, Duval also is home to x-rated movies and retailers, gay and lesbian coffee houses, transients, pickpockets, con artists and three-legged dogs pissing on fire hydrants. In other words, Key West paints a picture that fulfills a dream for us all. A few doors down from Caribbean Jewelry Company was a new fly fishing store. A two-story conch style wooded building painted yellow with white trim, I recognized the huge tarpon fly logo that filled the wooden sign out front. It was the same fly that was embroidered on my hat, my gift from Limbo. I went in to look around and see what was new in the world of fly fishing.

"Hello, welcome to The Saltwater Angler. I'm Jeffrey Cardenas. If I can help you, please let me know."

As Jeffrey and I talked, he gave me a tour. Proudly he showed me the many racks of fine fly rods, the showcase filled with better reels and his extensive collection of books for sale. The highly polished old oak wood floors creaked a little and upon the renovated walls hung many fine paintings of leaping tarpon and tailing bonefish.

Once again I found myself evaluating Jeffrey as if he were a customer. Jeffrey was a kind and polite man. Although he had a touch of gray in his hair, he was young; I guessed his age to be forty. He was honest and sincere. Jeffrey stood about six feet, had a friendly grin, a dark tan and eyes the color of fine aquamarine.

"Another benefit of growing up in the jewelry business," I thought.

One of the advantages of being raised the son of a jeweler was the great comparisons that gemstones provided. Great analogies often stuck in my imagination. The water was the color of fine Columbian emeralds. She wore a ruby-red gown. My tarpon's eye was light amber. I loved the sapphire-blue Gulf Stream. In this case, it was Jeffrey's aqua color eyes that added character to his being.

After about thirty minutes I felt like Jeffrey and I were old pals. He introduced me to everyone in the shop and I explained my plans to eventually guide in the Keys. Jeffrey used to guide before his retail business became so successful. He primarily chartered fly fishermen to the Marquesas in search of the big three: tarpon, permit and bonefish. He now sets up guides with charters. He told me that he would help me get started in the guiding business as soon as I was ready.

Jeffrey's store was fully equipped with all the better name brands that feed the fly fishing craze. Names such as Orvis, Sage, Abel, Loomis, Patagonia, Lamson, and Seamaster were a few that caught my eye. Above the store were guest house accommodations for up to six people. The two rooms, named The Bonefish Room and The Tarpon Room, shared a common kitchen area. The recreation area was great. Besides a big-screen television set and a first-rate stereo Jeffrey also had it equipped with a deluxe fly-fishing library and fly-tying benches. He supplied all the material to tie the one and only fly every angler needs for their day on the flats.

"As soon as you get settled with a job and a place to live give me a call, Powell," Jeffrey said. "I'll take you to the Marquesas and remind you just what it is that starts that saltwater flow through your veins."

I agreed it would be a day I would look forward to.

"Where ya staying now, Powell?"

"With a new friend of mine up on Sugarloaf," I replied.

"What's the phone up there?

When I told him, his eyes lit up and a big grin covered his face. He said, "That's Limbo's number."

"Yeah," I said, "That's who I'm staying with. I thought you probably knew him. A while back, he gave me one of your long billed fishing hats. I love it and he swears it's good luck. "

"You don't need me to show you the Keys, Powell. Limbo's the best guide these islands have ever seen. He taught me everything I know about fishing. He's a great guy, too."

"I'll tell you what, Jeffrey, if I get the job at the jewelry store, on the day before I start the three of us will go to the Marquesas, you, me and Limbo."

As I left the store, I was feeling good about life once again. I had two new friends and maybe a job. It was also good to know that Limbo had such a great reputation.

The sun was about to set. Dusk is always the perfect time of day to drive in the Keys. I stopped off at the M & M Laundry to get a large cup of con leche for the ride. This Cuban brew would eventually turn me into a coffeeholic. I guess there are worse things.

"Where the hell you been?" was my greeting when I finally arrived at Summerland. "We've got to get going, it's almost eight o'clock, and Frankie's only singing till nine-thirty," Limbo barked.

We jumped into the car and Limbo explained that on Thursday nights he always eats on Cudjoe Key. Thursdays at Coco's Cantina the special is fried grouper, black beans and yellow rice and plantains. Carlos and Flora, the owners, have live music on Thursday nights. Frankie Russell sings and plays old Patsy Cline songs till nine-thirty.

We got the only little table left, which happened to be in the corner near the stage. The music was loud and Frankie was playing her banjo and yodeling an old but somewhat familiar tune. There was a guitar player with a harmonica strapped around his neck like Bob Dylan. That was the band—two musicians.

"Como esta, Señor Limbo," an attractive waitress said as she handed him his nonalcoholic beer. "Would you like something to drink Señor?" she asked me.

"Yes, a Corona with lime, please."

"Bring us two specials to go with those beers, Flora, por favor," Limbo said.

Limbo explained that Carlos and Flora were from Nicaragua and were some of the best cooks in the Keys. The meal certainly backed him up. Everything was perfect.

Limbo said he had the recipe for the batter and seasoning on the grouper and would show me later.

"By the way, Powell, we can't go fishing tomorrow like we planned."

"Why not?" I said.

"Something came up," he said as he poured hot sauce from a

gallon jug over his beans and rice.

Frankie was in the middle of "Crazy" and doing a pretty good rendition. Everyone in the place was standing and singing along. Cudjoe Key was a happening town tonight. Limbo explained to me that Frankie used to commercial fish many, many years ago.

"That would explain her last song, about long-lining marlin in the Gulf Stream." I said.

"Frankie was married to Joe Russell. They owned a saloon in Key West so many years ago she'd like to forget. It's called Sloppy Joe's."

Of course I'd heard of Sloppy Joe's. It's a big attraction now on Duval Street. All the tourists go there to drink and buy T-shirts.

After telling me stories about fishing Cuba with Hemingway and why Hemingway's cats had so many toes, Limbo says, "Oh I forgot. Congratulations Powell! Or I think congratulations anyway."

"On what?" I said.

"You have a second interview at the jeweler's tomorrow. That's why we can't go fishing. Someone named Jennifer called and asked if you could be there tomorrow morning at seven forty-five. I told her you would be. "

"Great! Thanks, Limbo."

We had some flan, and con leche and told Carlos how much we enjoyed the meal. We left after Frankie finished her last song. It was obvious the lady enjoyed these Thursday nights.

I slept on and off all night. Butterflies in my stomach had me up well before the first ray of light beamed across the south end of Florida. Duval Street was put up for the evening. Although I had never visited the street at 5:30 a. m. , I imagined what it must be like. The last drunks had left Sloppy Joe's and Capt'n Tony's. The store fronts were all locked up and secured. No one was buying T-shirts, post cards or leather G-strings.

As the first sunlight spilled over the roof top of the Caribbean Jewelry Company, it lit up "Fast Buck Freddies" and all the storefronts on the west side. Tucked away in the shadows on the east side of Duval was a two-story yellow building that was owned and operated by a new friend.

The tourists were passed out in their motels. Bermuda shorts still snug around their waists. It was a great time of day. Quiet time, time to rest the brain, time to think.

I felt good about being called back, and was extra careful not to wake up Capain Limbo. He never had much good to say about Winston Sloan or the Caribbean Jewelry Company. Although he wasn't specific, I had the distinct feeling that ol' Limbo knew a little more about things than he let on. Maybe he didn't trust Sloan or maybe he didn't like him or whatever. At this point I didn't care. I needed some cash flow, a little income. I needed a job. Limbo's ulterior motives for my getting this job were not important now. I shaved twice, washed and dried my hair, pulled out a white, starched shirt with my most conservative tie and looked in the mirror. Charles, Sr. would have been proud, I thought aloud. Hell, I looked just like him.

At seven forty-three a.m., I entered the front door of The Caribbean Jewelry Company.

"Good morning, Powell. Mr. Sloan is waiting in his office," said Jennifer as I passed in front of the showcase that kept me from viewing her well shaped lower body.

"Thank you, Jennifer," I said as she directed me to the office door that read Winston L. Sloan, President.

"Come in, Charles. I'm very glad to see that you're punctual," said Sloan.

Winston Sloan was a fit man of about fifty years. At six-foot two, he was confident and sure of himself. I sensed that he liked being in control. He had dark, piercing eyes, neatly combed gray hair and no neck. He never smiled in my presence. Trying purposely not to evaluate Sloan, I found myself not liking him. I had no reason to feel this way. But, my first impressions were usually very accurate. In the days to come I would certainly realize why I felt apprehension.

"Thank you, sir, I always try my best to keep my appointments," I replied.

Being so nervous, I felt my stomach begin to knot up. I had to relax a little and calm down before I shit all over myself. I didn't want to seem too eager, yet I wanted him to know that I did, indeed, want to work for the Caribbean Jewelry Company.

"Tell me something Charles—"

"Excuse me, Mr. Sloan, but if you don't mind could you call me Powell? I go by my middle name, Powell."

"As I was saying, Charles, I mean, Powell, are you related to the Charles Taylor who is in the jewelry business in Gulf Breeze?"

I knew immediately he hadn't read my application or this was some kind of test. I had written on the job application my preferred name, who my parents were and my previous job at Taylor's Jewelry Company in Gulf Breeze, Florida.

"Yes, sir, he's my father."

"Very good," he said with a big grin that showed a lot of teeth and gums. "Your father and I met in Las Vegas a couple of years ago at a jewelry show. Very smart man, your father."

"Thank you, sir."

"Powell, I like you and want you to be a part of our store. However, I don't know much about your background or your ability. I'm told you are a gemologist with the GIA and that you have experience in appraising. What I've decided to do is to give you a piece of jewelry to appraise. If you satisfy me that you are experienced enough, I'll hire you on a trial basis for 90 days. If you prove yourself to be reliable, dedicated and knowledgeable, I'll make you assistant manager. If not, you'll be back on the street looking for a job. Is that satisfactory with you?"

I was deciding if I should play hard to get or jump at the offer when he said. "Powell, I need an answer now, either you want the job or you don't. What will it be?"

The intimidation factor worked a hundred percent. I belted out "Yes, sir, I'd love the chance to prove myself."

What a gay and stupid answer," I thought. If that wasn't bad enough, when I jumped up to shake Mr. Sloan's hand my twisted insides trapped an air pocket and squeezed it down and out the closest exit available. The result was a rip-roaring gas explosion. I had just farted on my future employer.

"Excuse me, sir, I am really nervous and I had too many beans with rice last night."

He just shook his head and smiled. I could not exit quickly enough. Tomorrow was Saturday and I was to begin work on Monday.

In the meantime I would see if Limbo and Jeffrey could fish

tomorrow, since they both shared a similar love for the Marquesas. That would give me all day Sunday to brush up on my jewelry appraising. I'm sure this would be a no brainer. Let's face it, how difficult could one appraisal be?

At four-thirty the next morning, Limbo and I met Jeffrey at Garrison Bight Marina where he keeps his skiff. The Keys restaurants had not yet opened their doors. It was too early, even, for an Egg McMuffin. As we sat on the dock eating day-old bagels and drinking instant coffee, Jeffrey told Limbo he was happy I had asked him to fish today. We talked for a few moments, ate and rigged our tackle. Today's forecast called for clear, sunny skies with a high of eighty-eight. As I strung the fly line through the eyes of my rod, I noticed the stars were so bright they looked close enough to touch. Garrison Bight was serene and quiet. There was no chatter from the laughing gulls that would soon inhabit the air. There were no outboards coughing and spitting out water as there soon would be. Colorful reflections from nearby signs covered the surface of the black waters in the marina. On the edge of the Bight I could distinguish the big red star with a green background that was being illuminated by the Texaco signage across the boulevard. It was a happy reunion between old friends as we loaded gear aboard Jeffrey's sixteen-foot Maverick Mirage. The one thing I always noticed about Keys guides is the manifest respect they have for each other. I knew I could learn a great deal from these two pros.

"So you're still slipping over there before sunup?" Limbo asked Jeffrey.

"Sure am," he replied. "The best tarpon fishing around this area happens right about daylight on the northeast side of the Marquesas. Besides, I usually have them to myself for a couple of hours before the other skiffs show up."

Jeffrey had spent many hours practicing the run between the flats of Key West and the atoll called the Marquesas. To maneuver a boat, even a shallow water skiff, through such treacherous bottoms was an amazing feat during daylight hours. To accomplish it in total darkness seemed almost magic.

With the light of the moon rippling in our wake, the three of us sat in the dark, two feet from the deafening roar of ninety horses. As I was sitting there in total obscurity, speeding through a world I could not see, I remembered a conversation I had with Jeffrey on the day we met. His stories about the Marquesas were pleasantly planted in my head. At the height of his guiding career Jeffrey spent between two fifty to two hundred seventy days a year on the water, with the majority of these days in the Marquesas. He remembered days when huge sawfish laid up in the channel, motionless on the southeast corner. His musings took him back to a time when Cuban refugees drifted with Caribbean currents in search of freedom in a new land. And the days when modern-day pirates smuggled everything from dope to refugees to earn a quick buck. "At one time," he said, "abandoned boats littered the Marquesas Isles like rusty cans on the side of a busy highway."

My butt muscle relaxed slightly as Jeffrey pulled back on the throttle, slowing the boat to an idle. I told him I felt a little uneasy, speeding through the night with all of those unmarked buoys, boats, crab traps, and chunks of driftwood zipping past us.

"Not to worry," he said. "I've done this before."

Jeffrey's time spent alone in the Marquesas showed that he had great respect for the environment.

"The Marquesas is the only atoll in the Atlantic. It was formed not by a volcano, but possibly by a prehistoric meteor," said Jeffrey.

Jeffrey is enchanted by the Marquesas. He told us about secret passageways in the mangroves that few humans have ever seen. He relived, with such emotion, his first grand slam in this great refuge. For a Keys guide, catching a grand slam is a remarkable feat, one that Jeffrey has done many times over.

Offshore, blue water grand slams are when an angler catches a blue marlin, white marlin and sailfish all in the same day. On the flats and in these Marquesas, the angler who successfully lands a bonefish, tarpon and permit on the same outing has reason to brag on his grand slam. Add a mutton snapper and you have accomplished a super slam. Still idling through the channels, Jeffrey continued to mesmerize us with stories of the Marquesas.

He pointed out all of the natural vegetation to the area. He loved the wildlife that made a home here.

"That spot over there is one of the only places in the world that the magnificent Frigate bird actually breeds," he said as he pointed across the stern.

"Hey, look up ahead of us," Limbo said. "Those are my favorite birds that fly."

With their distinctive white feathers and long, thin, curved pinkish bills, even I recognized them as white ibis.

"Do they nest and breed in the Marquesas also?" I asked.

"No they just visit here. I've never seen them nest in this area." Jeffrey said.

Limbo then decided to tell us why they don't nest in the Marquesas mangroves.

"White ibis," he explained in his professor's voice, "continually change their colony sites and often migrate considerable distances. Their main prey is small crustaceans that are found in the ever-changing shallows. However, because of the salt content, young birds do not develop properly on brackish-water prey. Ibis must have freshwater feeding sites for successful breeding. The Marquesas do not have any natural freshwater sources. I believe ibis breed from South Carolina and all through Florida. I think they also nest in Cuba and Jamaica."

"Thank you, Mr. Audubon," I chimed.

"Please, Powell, don't compare me with James Audubon. I'm afraid he and I wouldn't see eye-to-eye if he were still alive."

I knew what ol' Limbo was getting at. However, I didn't pursue the issue. I figured I'd leave that story for him to tell later. I had read a bit about Audubon in school. He was not the conservationist the world viewed him to be. He killed for sport and amusement. He also killed birds to use as dead models for his art. That's the reason for the lifeless poses most of his birds display. He killed hundreds of Florida birds each day. So I looked forward to Limbo's version of Audubon's life. One day soon, when I might not be as satisfied and content with life, I would ask Limbo to explain himself.

The one-hour skiff ride west to the Marquesas was intriguing. I have often studied the charts between Key West and the Marquesas. The fact that we ran wide open through "The Lakes," a series of shallow lagoons protected by islands and the reef, intrigued me the most. Although pitch black dark, I could sense the skinny waters beneath us as we passed the wrecked boats and abandoned lobster traps, on the shallows of Woman and Man Keys.

When we approached the choppy waters of Boca Grande channel, Jeffrey never slowed down. We entered the ball busting channel at fifty miles per hour. Now that was an exciting ten minute run, bouncing up and down on my assbone in a two to three-foot chop unable to even see the bow of the boat, it was so dark. Limbo called it exhilarating. Jeffrey thought of it as an adventure. I knew it was dumb as shit. The sun was barely peeking over the horizon as Jeffrey cut the engine and climbed up on the poling platform.

"Hey, Jeffrey," I said, "why don't you take off a month or so and live out here? You could write a book on the Marquesas while you fish and enjoy life. It's obvious you probably know as much about the area as anyone."

"Maybe one day," he replied.

I thought I heard him then mumble something about a time and place with fish. When I asked what he had said, he just smiled and said "Yeah, one day, maybe."

Jeffrey spotted a school of large, rolling tarpon on the edge of a channel about three hundred fifty yards down wind. The radio weather report had changed its earlier forecast to include a wind at twenty-five knots. It was an accurate report. With the wind and the current both howling Jeffrey said: "Both of ya'll get your lines stripped out and ready. You're only going to get one chance, so whatever you do, don't fuck up."

He grinned from ear to ear.

I felt my knees knocking together, so I took a deep breath. I realized this tarpon fever was indeed addictive. But today we would win. Let's face it, I thought, how could we not hook up. Two of the best fishermen in the Keys were putting me right in the center of Tarpon-ville. Besides I had already landed my first "poon." I was already a pro.

"With these turbulent winds and currents we'll drift through the school and take our best shots," Jeffrey explained. "As soon as we get through the channel I'll have to start the engine to keep from drifting up on the flat."

When the fish were about one hundred feet from the boat, Limbo and I both were about to cast. I raised my rod tip about the same time a gust of wind blew my line around Limbo's. It wasn't just a tangle, but rather the worst knot you could imagine. Well, we floated right through the huge school of tarpon as Jeffrey and the fish laughed aloud. Limbo and I were not quite as amused. We watched as about fifty tarpon in the one hundred-pound class swam all around the boat.

Jeffrey said, "Don't feel bad, Powell, this is one of those times when the fish wins."

He smiled. We didn't. Jeffrey started the engine and idled out of the channel as we all had a good laugh.

Limbo started up the conversation again, I think just to put me at ease.

"The fish may have won, but we were a close second, Powell. Besides, it's good to lose occasionally."

"Yeah, why's that Limbo," I said.

He looked at Jeffrey, then me and said, "It makes you appreciate the wins more."

By the time we headed east to Key West that afternoon, we had seen all the sights that send your blood rushing to your head. We jumped tarpon, caught bonefish and spooked three schools of large permit. As soon as I organized my life, the elusive permit would be the object of my hunt. This day in the Marquesas taught me a new-found respect for this fish that looks like a round, silver platter. A huge pompano, the permit tests every skillful trick an angler knows. Try catching one on a fly rod and your chances become nearly impossible. I would research this great fish and target him at a later date.

"Jeffrey, did you hear that Powell got a job down the road from you?" Limbo asked.

"Where's that?" Jeffrey replied.

"Caribbean Jewelers," I said before Limbo had a chance to answer. Jeffrey's obvious pause led me to believe he did not fully approve. He merely wished me the best of luck in my new job and hoped it would accelerate my plan to guide in the Keys. Jeffrey is a gentleman. I suspect he would have liked to say more on the subject, but was too kind.

Chapter Seven ——

Sugarloaf Key is almost the exact distance east from Key West as the Marquessas are west. The good side of that is I had thirty minutes of brain time during my drive to work. The bad side is that there are occasions when you can think about things too much.

On this particular morning, the Monday I started my new job, my mind was consumed with appraising. My father had taught me the importance of good appraising. He said that for a long time, ethical jewelers refused to do appraisals on any new merchandise they did not sell. These jewelers thought that if an appraisal was higher than the customer paid, the buyer would think that the jeweler was overpriced. If the appraised price was lower, it could offend a competitor and cause friction in the trade, or between the trade and the public. Besides, most often the customer blames the jeweler who made the appraisal. Buyers don't want to admit they paid too much money for their jewelry. Charles Sr. used to compare it to the days of kings and knights. "The messenger who brought bad news was often killed," he would say.

Although as a jeweler, you are only reporting what you see and know, you can still be held responsible in the eyes of the customer. Their fears of legal entanglements were also reason enough for many jewelers to refuse appraisal work. However, as Dad always said, if you're honest in life and business, you'll have no problems.

The pressure of having to impress Mr. Sloan with my ability did not bother me as much as wondering if we shared the same values. If not, I thought, this first day may be my last.

I was a little nervous as I arrived at the shop door a few minutes early. Jennifer unlocked the door and let me in.

"Good morning, Powell. It's great to see you again."

"Thanks, Jennifer, I'm glad to be here," I said.

She directed me to Mr. Sloan's office. He came in shortly after and seemed quite cordial, yet very professional. Sloan's three piece suit was blue with thin pin stripes. Conservative. The scent of his after shave was a bit too overwhelming this early in the morning. Glancing down at his shoes I noticed something peculiar. His black alligator shoes did not match his brown leather belt. I wanted to smile but, naturally, did not. As if he were reading my mind Sloan said, "I lost my black belt somewhere. "

His attitude was too cocky; he was too alert. I did not look up and did not answer him. The fact is, I did not like Sloan.

He told me it would probably take me all day to finish the appraisal, and that definitely caught my attention. Until now the longest I had ever spent appraising a single piece of jewelry was about two hours. It was a ladies platinum and 18 karat gold choker necklace that had more than five hundred stones in it. Most of the diamonds were different shapes and sizes. The emeralds, rubies, and sapphires in the neckpiece were all high quality, like the diamonds—the best. After grading color, clarity, and cut on all five hundred or so stones, I thought my eyes were going to drop out of their sockets. "What on earth could possibly take eight hours to appraise?" I thought.

"Let me ask you a question, Powell, before you get started."

"Yes, sir," I replied.

"What do you think about appraising, Powell? I mean, do you think it's a good idea for us to do appraisals on all kinds of jewelry?" he said.

Not really sure if this was a trick question, I decided to answer it, remembering Charles Sr.'s philosophy. I said, "Well Mr. Sloan, here's the way I view appraising. Ah, since you asked, sir, I feel that an honest jeweler who charges a reasonable markup will not be annoyed at having his prices confirmed. A competitor operating on a legitimate markup would rarely be undersold anyway. An average person would rather deal with the jeweler whose knowledge of jewelry and prices can be trusted. I feel that there is no activity in a jewelry store more important than good appraising and nothing that builds customers' confidence more."

There was a long intimidating pause. However, I felt relaxed and confident for the first time. Winston Sloan knew how I felt now. If he didn't like it, now was the time to remedy it. I was being honest.

"Perfect answer, Powell," Sloan muttered. He then directed me to the gem lab where I would do the work. It was quite impressive, with its state-of-the-art grading equipment: microscopes, color graders, refractive index machines, polariscopes, proportion scopes, digital scales, charts, videos and a complete library on gemstones and diamonds. Everything was clean and white. There was no phone and no windows, no interruptions and nothing to interfere with my concentration. If a window were present, I might be tempted to daydream and watch the Conch Train slither back and forth down the street like a huge snake doing the Conga. I first rode on the Conch Tour Train when I was eight years old. A Willis Jeep, dressed up like a locomotive engine, pulled a string of trailing cars filled with attentive tourists through the old town of Cayo Huesto. In the caboose, so many years ago, were Charles Sr., Imogene, Bradford, and Powell Taylor. I love this old town.

As Mr. Sloan handed me a large wooden case, he said, "Powell, here is the item for you to appraise. I designed it and two of my jewelers made it. It took them more than a year to complete and I've never taken the time to figure its value. I would like you to be as concise and accurate as possible. You don't have to put a price on it. In fact, I'm not sure you can put a price on it."

Right then I knew I would have to place a dollar amount at the end of my appraisal. I felt challenged and would not let Sloan prove my incompetence.

"I'll leave you with it, Powell. Have fun," he said as he closed the door behind him.

I removed the lid from the box. I was very impressed. It was the most breathtaking array of gold and jewels I'd ever witnessed. For an instant, I envisioned it in some museum in New York City. Honestly, I had not thought much of Caribbean Jewelers until this moment. In all the visits I'd made to the store, including this one, I had yet to see a customer. Surely anyone capable of creating such a piece of art must have a successful business. The metal plate attached to the wood base read, *The Reef.*

I took out my pen and notebook, gathered my calculator and millimeter gauge. I began. I measured, estimated and graded gold content and stone identifications for more than four hours. I then went back through all my notes and scribbling and typed it out on the computer. I tried to be as accurate and concise as Mr. Sloan expected. After another two hours I proudly read over my completed report as the computer spit it out.

Caribbean Jewelry Company
Key West Florida

GEMOLOGIST

DIAMOND
MERCHANTS

**JEWELRY
APPRAISAL**   PROPERTY OF_____ Mr. Winston L. Sloan _____

ADDRESS_____

Key West, Florida

These estimated replacement costs are based only on estimates of the quality of the stones (unless specifically stated that the stones were removed and graded) We assume no liability with respect to any action that may be taken on the basis of the appraisal.

ITEM	ARTICLE	IDENTIFYING DESCRIPTION	VALUE
1 REEF		One (1) Handmade three-dimensional underwater scene with coral reef, tropical fish, sea life and sunken ship motif. An assortment of metals used include: 14 karat yellow gold; 14K white gold; 18K yellow gold; 18K white gold and platinum (10% iridium). The sculptured art is mounted on a beveled red mahogany base one inch thick measuring 16 inches by 9 inches. The base contains a 14K yellow gold plate 1mm thick, 2 inches by 1 inch and is hand engraved in script lettering as follows: "The Reef" Designed By Winston L. Sloan	

hereby certify that the above named person has submitted the above listed articles for appraisal and that the values indicated are in accordance with my best knowledge and belief as of this date.

Date_____   _____ **Appraiser**

C. Powell Taylor

Address_____

Gemologist

Caribbean Jewelry Company
Key West Florida

GEMOLOGIST

DIAMOND MERCHANTS

JEWELRY APPRAISAL

PROPERTY OF_____ Mr. Winston L. Sloan _____

ADDRESS_____

_____

ITEM	ARTICLE	IDENTIFYING DESCRIPTION	VALUE
1 REEF (cont.)		The total measurements of the sculpture, excluding the base, are: Height: 9.65 inches Width: 13.25 inches Depth: 7.29 inches The weights (estimated from measurements and calculations are as follows: 14K yellow gold: 503.30 grams 14K white gold: 76.0 grams 18K yellow gold: 49.1 grams 18K white gold: 50.10 grams Platinum: 18.56 grams Total weight is approximately 697 grams (converted equals 22.42 troy ounces or 1.867 troy pounds). Starting at left side when viewing from front the piece contains: One 14K yellow gold sunken treasure chest with hinged 18K white gold lid and trim, measuring 26.2mm X 13.4mm; attached to the chest is a 14K yellow gold octopus with .02 cts. full cut diamond eyes: Inside the chest is an assortment of 14K and 18K yellow gold chains and bars. Next is: Two 14K yellow gold brain corals measuring two inches in diameter each. 14K white gold coral rock 2.75 inches by 1.5 inches with 18K yellow gold stone crab with matches 2mm ruby eyes; behind this is a 14K yellow gold sea fan 5 inches X 4 inches X 1.2 mm thick; next is a 18K yellow gold branch coral 6 inches high with a 3mm diameter trunk; atop the coral is a 14K yellow gold manta ray, with four, 18K yellow gold Queen Triggerfish swimming throughout coral branches. On the right side in the rear section there is one set of 14K yellow gold sea weed (four strands) measuring 5mm X 1mm thick X 5 inches high;	

hereby certify that the above named person has submitted the above listed articles for appraisal and that the values indicated are in accordance with my best knowledge and belief as of this date.

Date _____

_____ **Appraiser**

Address _____

C. Powell Taylor

Gemologist

$\mathcal{C}aribbean$ Jewelry Company
Key West Florida

GEMOLOGIST

DIAMOND
MERCHANTS

**JEWELRY
APPRAISAL**   PROPERTY OF___Mr. Winston L. Sloan_____

ADDRESS_____

ITEM	ARTICLE	IDENTIFYING DESCRIPTION	VALUE
1	REEF (cont.)	One set 18K white gold sea weed (three strands) measuring 7mm X 1mm X 6 1/2 inches high.	

One set 18K white gold sea weed (three strands) measuring 7mm X 1mm X 6 1/2 inches high.

    One large 14K and 18K yellow gold (mixed) coral rock with assorted gold shells (conch, wentle traps, sandollars, starfish, snails and sea biscuits). One large 14K yellow gold oyster shell one and a half X 1", hinged with one 7 mm cultured gray pearl glued on post inside: two sets of 14K yellow gold tube sponges with natural 3.5 mm rubies set in tops, next to 18K yellow gold branch coral 3 inches high X 2 inches wide with 3.5 mm stalks; next to 18K yellow gold tubular coral 2 inches X 1.5 inches with platinum and 18K yellow gold bezels containing diamonds and emeralds. The front center contains various 14K and 18K yellow gold fossilized design coral with impressions on both, extinct fish, shrimp and sea roaches. 14K yellow gold large surface area (3 inches in diameter) containing 14K yellow gold "purple sponge," with 14K yellow gold lobster, sea biscuits and whelks, with one 14K white gold anchor and one 18K white gold sun - starfish measuring 28 mm from tip to tip of rays:

    Left front contains:

    One large 14K yellow gold handmade hull and bow section of old Spanish galleon. Total length is 9.0 inches and 3.1 inches wide, 2.25 inches deep. Weight of the boat only is approximately 111 grams. Main mast and crow's nest is 9 inches high with 6 mm tapered 14K yellow gold tubing (to 3 mm). Hand carved mermaid figurehead with natural ruby eyes; masts are all bezel set with natural diamonds, emeralds, sapphires and rubies: The total weight of stones and their grades are as follows:

    Rubies:
    8-round faceted natural rubies (corrundum) at 1.25mm
    5-round faceted natural rubies (corrundum) at 2.0mm
    7-round faceted natural rubies (corrundum) at 2.5mm

hereby certify that the above named person has submitted the above listed articles for appraisal and that the values indicated are in accordance with my best knowledge and belief as of this date.

Date_____   _____ Appraiser

Address_____   C. Powell Taylor

Gemologist

GEMOLOGIST

Caribbean Jewelry Company
Key West Florida

DIAMOND MERCHANTS

JEWELRY APPRAISAL

PROPERTY OF __Mr. Winston L. Sloan__

ADDRESS _____

ITEM	ARTICLE	IDENTIFYING DESCRIPTION	VALUE
1	REEF (cont.)	20-round faceted natural rubies (corrundum) at 2.75mm 1-round faceted natural ruby (corrundum) at 3.5mm very fine quality Hue - slpR Tone - 6 Intensity - 4 Sapphires: 9-round faceted natural blue sapphires (corrundum) at 2.0mm 11-round faceted natural blue sapphires (corrundum) at 2.5mm 20-round faceted natural blue sapphires (corrundum) at 3.0mm 2-round faceted natural blue sapphires (corrundum) at 3.5mm very fine quality Hue - B Tone - 5 Intensity - 6 Emeralds: 20-round faceted natural emeralds (beryl) at 1.0mm 6-round faceted natural emeralds (beryl) at 2.5mm 20-round faceted natural emeralds (beryl) at 3.0mm 1-round faceted natural emerald (beryl) at 3.5mm very fine quality Hue - bG Tone - 5 Intensity - 5 Diamonds:	

hereby certify that the above named person has submitted the above listed articles for appraisal and that the values indicated are in accordance with my best knowledge and belief as of this date.

)ate _____ _____ Appraiser

C. Powell Taylor

Address _____

Gemologist

Caribbean Jewelry Company
Key West Florida

GEMOLOGIST

DIAMOND MERCHANTS

JEWELRY APPRAISAL

PROPERTY OF___Mr. Winston L. Sloan_____

ADDRESS_____

These estimated replacement costs are based only on estimates of the quality of the stones (unless specifically stated that the stones were removed and graded). We assume no liability with respect to any action that may be taken on the basis of the appraisal.

ITEM	ARTICLE	IDENTIFYING DESCRIPTION	VALUE
1	REEF (cont.)	18-round full cut diamonds at .01cts. 22-round full cut diamonds at .02cts. 2-round full cut diamonds at .03cts. 3-round full cut diamonds at .04cts. 6 round full cut diamonds at .05cts. color - G clarity - VS1 to VS2 1-round brilliant cut diamond at approximately 1.65cts. (estimated by measurements) color - G clarity - VVS2 culet - medium girdle - medium finish and symmetry - good polish - very good 1 - Round brilliant cut diamond at approximately 1.01cts. (estimated by measurements) color - H clarity - VS2 culet - small to medium girdle - thin to thick, faceted finish and symmetry - fair polish - good 6 - Round brilliant cut diamonds at approximately .25cts. each. (estimated by measurements)	

hereby certify that the above named person has submitted the above listed articles for appraisal and that the values indicated are in accordance with my best knowledge and belief as of this date.

Date_____

Address_____

_____ **Appraiser**

C. Powell Taylor

Gemologist

Caribbean Jewelry Company
Key West Florida

GEMOLOGIST

DIAMOND MERCHANTS

JEWELRY APPRAISAL

PROPERTY OF___Mr. Winston L. Sloan_____

ADDRESS_____

_____

These estimated replacement costs are based only on estimates of the quality of the stones (unless specifically stated that the stones were removed and graded). We assume no liability with respect to any action that may be taken on the basis of the appraisal.

ITEM	ARTICLE	IDENTIFYING DESCRIPTION	VALUE
1	REEF (cont.)	color - H clarity - SI1 culet - med. to large girdle - medium finish and symmetry - fair to good polish - good	
		REPLACEMENT VALUE	$195,000.00

hereby certify that the above named person has submitted the above listed articles for appraisal and that the values indicated are in accordance with my best knowledge and belief as of this date.

Date_____

Address_____

_____ Appraiser

C. Powell Taylor

Gemologist

I was proud of the final product. After calculating it all and figuring labor expenses I added a twenty percent profit and wrote down the replacement value of *The Reef.*

One hundred ninety-five-thousand dollars looked as impressive as the description that preceded it. I felt I was accurate. Winston (I was now on a first name basis, in my mind at least) would have to agree with my conclusion.

I was sitting there admiring my work, when the door opened and Jennifer stuck her head in and said. "Powell, you getting hungry in here?"

I looked at my watch. It was almost six p. m. The store closed at five-thirty.

"As a matter of fact, Jennifer, I just finished and I'm starving to death. Would you like to get a bite to eat after you lock up?" I said.

"Sure!" she replied.

As Jennifer was closing up, I made an extra copy of the appraisal for myself, placed it in my notebook. I would send it to Charles, Sr. later. Maybe he would be proud, and maybe not. He wasn't much for compliments.

I put the original copy on Winston's, or rather, Mr. Sloan's desk so he could see it first thing in the morning. I almost couldn't wait till tomorrow to get his reaction. I felt good and was sure that Tuesday probably would bring well-earned compliments and accolades. I was feeling a little cocky, but what the hell? I thought.

As Jennifer locked the front door, I realized I hadn't even noticed how great she looked today. She was wearing a white mini-skirt with no hose. Her legs were nicely tanned and very pleasant looking. Things were going so well, I dreamed for a moment that I might even get laid. What a day, I imagined— A perfect job on my task of appraising and then ending the day by slipping under the sheets with gorgeous Jennifer.

It didn't exactly work out that way. In fact, the whole time we were walking to the restaurant, she was telling me not to get any ideas.

"I don't date employees, Powell," she said. "It's not a good idea, and I don't think Mr. Sloan would approve. I'm just taking you to dinner as a friend in a new job."

"I understand completely, Jennifer," I said as I was undressing her with my eyes. Of course I was lying, I didn't understand at all.

All she could talk about at dinner was her damned cat named Hemingway. I got the feeling that the only pussy of Jennifer's I would ever see would be Hemingway.

It turned out to be a pleasant evening after all. Feasting on a great Cuban meal at Jose's, we walked over to Mallory Square and sat on the dock. The sun had already set, allowing the tourists to return to their haunts on Duval Street. We talked for hours under the moonlight. I now felt badly about my earlier thoughts. Jennifer was quite a nice lady.

Hemingway was a direct descendant of one of the original cats that lived with ol' Ernest so many years ago.

"Does he have extra toes?" I asked, trying to influence her with my new knowledge.

"Yes, he does, Powell! How in the world did you know that?" she asked.

I figured now was my chance. I explained to her that my mother loves cats and that I read up on them one time. Girls love it when you talk about your Mama. Throw in a little pet talk and I just might get laid after all.

"The reason Hemingway's cats have extra toes is a really interesting story. Have you ever heard it, Jennifer?" I asked.

"Please Powell, call me Jenny, and no, I never did really understand that."

Jenny looked so pretty under the moonlight. I began to think of Dawn and how I missed her.

I continued my story to the best of my recollection of Limbo's version. I hated to tell her that although Hemingway had more than fifty cats while he lived in Cuba, he only had two of the pesky little felines when he lived in Key West. I also hated to tell her that cats with extra toes were no more than a product of mutant genes. I did tell her that the two cats Ernie brought to Key West probably were from the original brood in Cuba. However, I didn't have a clue if they were or not. After all, It sounded a mite more romantic.

"Jenny, did you know that your Hemingway is polydactyl?" I said.

"What?"

"Yeah," I continued, "he is in a ten percent minority of all cats. Normally, cats have five toes on each front foot and four on their back feet. When a cat such as ol' Hemingway has extra toes, it's called polydactyl."

I was on a roll and had her complete attention. I sure hoped Limbo hadn't made up all of this shit.

"Polydactyl cats come in all colors and sizes." I continued. "Your Hemingway is probably a descendant of the first six-toed cat a ship captain gave Ernest way back when. About half of the fifty or sixty cats at Hemingway's house, over on Whitehead Street, had extra toes."

"How many toes can they have?" Jenny asked.

"If I remember correctly, the maximum is seven toes on each foot. I believe some have even had twenty-eight toes total."

I then told her how unique and special her kitty was. I also told her that it was a fact that cats with extra toes were more amusing, fun and are inclined to love their owners more. It was complete bullshit, but sure sounded good. I had impressed her and had her confidence now.

"How about I take you home and you can introduce me to your little pussy?" I said with a little smile. Jenny definitely was not amused.

"You're just like all guys. You're disgusting, Powell. I was just starting to think you might be different. I thought you were compassionate and understanding. I actually thought you were interested in me and my kitty. You're OBSCENE, Powell. Take me home now."

"I just capsized and drowned in my own stupidity," I thought. No other words came from her lips the remainder of the evening.

After saying good night to the wall, I had thirty minutes to realize my mistake, before I arrived at Limbo's home. Somehow I started thinking of synonyms for obscene. In Jenny's mind I was obscene, offensive, atrocious, disgusting, evil, foul, hideous, horrible, horrid, loathsome, nasty, nauseating, noisome, repugnant, repulsive, revolting, sickening, crude, dirty, filthy, gross, rank, vulgar and vile. I was truly indecent this night. Obscene, what a great word, I thought. This reminded me of the word games our family used to play in the car to pass the time quickly as we crossed these very same bridges. The time indeed passed quickly. It was two thirty in the morning when I reached Limbo's. The house lights were all on and he was taking his nightly swim.

"He ain't right," I thought as I relaxed my head on the pillow. This had been one lengthy day!

Chapter Eight

After six weeks of hard work, long hours and dedicated sweat and toil, I had earned the respect of most of my fellow co-workers. Jenny and I were back to normal and getting along quite well once again. It took a lot of cat talk, but it was worth the effort. The only two employees who seemed not to like me were Mr. Sloan and Harrison Gray.

Mr. Gray, head of security for the store, was not a likeable sort in the first place. He appeared to be the solemn, serious, quiet and mysterious type. With his manicured fingernails, he showed up pressed, ironed, creased and ready. Ready for just what, I wasn't sure. His type thought those ten pedicured digits with that clear polish, looked so masculine. He was tall, pale and a little overweight. His dark black hair was slicked down and parted in the center of his head. A hairdo the young teens refer to as a butt cut, for obvious reasons.

Mr. Sloan, on the other hand, never got over the fact that I priced *The Reef* so accurately on my appraisal.

"A hundred and ninety five-thousand dollars is absurd and

ridiculously low, Powell. Besides, I told you not to price it.

"Are you always in a habit of disobeying orders on your first day at work?"

Those were exactly his words to me six weeks ago. After a month and a half of ass kissing he still did not seem at ease with me. I found out later from Jenny that once he had sold *The Reef* to a customer for seven hundred fifty thousand dollars. After some kind of problem the man returned it. I thought maybe Mr. Sloan was still upset because *The Reef* was returned. But, Jenny said he was never upset at the fact it was returned. I remember thinking he must have a better business than I even imagined. If I owned a store and a customer returned a piece of jewelry for three quarters of a million dollars, I'd cry for weeks.

The one big question I still had was, how on earth could he sell this gold mass of underwater scenes for three and a half times its worth. I know for a fact my appraisal was accurate. Why did Mr. Sloan and Mr. Gray detest me so?

It may well have been that I was just a little paranoid about these two guys. A couple of weeks earlier Limbo had finally spilled his guts and told me why he got me this job. It seems that Winston Sloan was being secretly investigated by local customs and the Miami authorities. Limbo was trying to be cautious and didn't want to tell me too much at first.

"Look Limbo, if you've got me in the middle of some shaky predicament, I want to know what's going on. I'm only going to help you if you level with me," I said. "I'm grateful to you for getting me this job. But I can't help if I don't know all the facts."

After about three hours of listening to his explanation, I had a hollow, sick feeling in the pit of my stomach. If Limbo was correct, I was working for a murderer.

Winston Sloan's partner in the jewelry store had mysteriously disappeared on a fishing trip in the Bahamas five years before.

"His body has never shown up and no one has heard from him since," said Limbo.

"The last time anyone saw him, he was fishing off Deep Water Cay in the Bahamas. Some native Bahamians found his boat washed aground the next day. Although there was no evidence of foul play, things didn't fit right." When I asked why he was so convinced that Mr. Sloan was guilty he just said, "Because."

It took another hour to learn that Mr. Sloan's partner had left his widow about ten million dollars. He also had a contract with Winston Sloan that stated: "In the event of one of the partners' death, the remaining stock and all assets of Caribbean Jewelry Co. would go to the surviving partner."

"So why do you think it was Mr. Sloan, Limbo?" I asked. "I mean, it seems like his widow had more of a motive than Sloan."

"That's a good question, Powell, but I've got a very good answer. The dead man and his wife were very much in love and were always seen together at all the Key West social functions. They were on the board of the local bank. They were active in the Hemingway Days celebration as well as Fantasy Fest. They both donated much time and money to charity organizations. They were inseparable. They even fished and dove together."

"Why didn't she go to the Bahamas on the trip that he disappeared?" I asked.

"Rumor has it that she wanted to, but it was a guys' trip. Guess what other guy went along?" Limbo asked.

"My boss?"

"Exactly."

"That's interesting all right, but I still think the widow is a suspect," I said, as if I were Sherlock Holmes.

"There's another reason why we don't suspect his widow, Powell. She has offered a two million-dollar reward for information leading to a conviction of her husband's murderer."

"Two million dollars?" I yelled. "You have to be kidding!"

"Yeah, I guess she figured she can spend twenty percent of her inheritance and still live pretty comfortably on the remaining eight mill. Besides, she has always suspected Winston Sloan.

What we want, Powell, is this. Keep an eye out on everything and everyone who enters the store. Keep your ears open for anything. Be nosey, be suspicious, but be careful. If Sloan is what we think he is, he wouldn't hesitate to kill you."

Customs and Limbo both thought that Mr. Sloan, along with his partner, had some type of scam going on together. They now feel that something went wrong or maybe that one partner wanted out. If so, that may be the reason he was now a silent partner.

I started to tell Limbo everything I knew about things thus far when I suddenly realized, "No wonder you're so interested in this, Limbo," I said. "Two million dollars! You want the two million bucks."

"Of course I do, Powell, but it'll only be one million for me."

"Why's that?" I asked.

"Cause if you do your job, like I think you will, you'll get the other million."

"No shit?" I blurted out.

"Yeah, Powell, no shit," Limbo replied.

"With that kinda money you can guide where and when you feel like it. You also can hire your own captain to take you fishing. In any case, you'll be able to pick and choose your guide or angler. If you're guiding some jerk who aggravates you, just escort him back to the dock and kick his ass out. You surely won't need his money."

I thought for a moment how nice it would be to fish and guide because I wanted to, not because I had to.

I finished telling Limbo the whole inside scoop on Caribbean Jewelers. I told him I wouldn't be surprised if Harrison Gray played some part in the game. Limbo was interested in my story, and especially in Harrison Gray and the seven hundred fifty thousand dollar *Reef* that was returned.

"Try to find out who bought it and why they returned it," he said.

I was nervous after Limbo and I talked. One minute I was spending my million. The next minute I feared for my life.

I decided to use the remainder of the afternoon to make some phone calls, first to Gulf Breeze. It was good to talk to Mom, Dad, and Brad. Everyone was doing fine and missed me, they said. I told Dad the amount of money *The Reef* had sold for. He was shocked.

"Son, if you think it is worth one hundred ninety-five thousand dollars, stick to it. Don't let them make you put a fictitious price on it, for any reason. I know you have the knowledge and expertise to make an accurate appraisal. Stick to your story, son," Charles Sr. said. "You're good at your job, just remember that."

It was as close to a compliment as I had ever received from him.

"Thanks, Dad, I will." I said before I hung up. I was still a little homesick for my family and my old lifestyle in Gulf Breeze. Between the letters and the phone calls, we kept in touch. We had some type of correspondence every week. They always knew my plans and what was going on in my life. However, somehow I neglected to tell them the Jenny and her Pussy story. Although an amusing story at the time, it now merely served as a lesson learned.

I next pulled out the latest letter from Boca Grande. Enclosed was a photo of Dawn with a huge snook. She said she caught it in "our fishing hole." She looked as beautiful as I remembered. In the short time I had been in the Keys, she had written me about twenty letters. I'd answered about half. I owed her one.

After writing her a long, detailed letter about my life in the Keys, I ended with my usual salutation. I invited her to come down and live with me. I told her I was going house shopping soon and she could help me decorate. I also told her that not a day had gone by that I didn't think of her. I did not lie. I truly hoped that some day we could journey through life together.

I tried to call her, but there was no answer. The message on her machine would tell her, "Miss you madly, Dawn, hope to see you again soon. Love and kisses."

Tomorrow was Monday. This would be my first Monday off since our new schedules. I now had Sundays and Mondays off. Two days in a row would be a pleasant change.

The seven weeks with Limbo were entertaining to say the least, but it was time for me to get a place of my own. Both of us could use the privacy and freedom, and I hoped that as soon as I got a place, Dawn would come visit. I wanted my new address to bring her south. Tomorrow was an important day for me. I would find a home.

"Remember what I told you, Powell. Don't let them intimidate you or rush you into buying a house today. Don't be in a hurry."

Those were Limbo's last instructions as I drove off that morning. They stuck in my mind.

I arrived at Sugarloaf Residential Properties, Inc. at least a good fifteen minutes early.

After a one-hour Keys real estate seminar given me by Captain Limbo recently, I knew how to play this new version of monopoly.

It was my time to buy. We studied the tide charts and made my appointments to view the waterfront homes at low tide. After a lifetime surrounded by water I knew that life was much more beautiful at high tide. It was an optimistic tide, I thought. It's clear, brilliant water, full of life forms that always gives me a feeling of living in a clean, fresh, problem-free world.

Low tide strips away the high-tide facade. When the tide is out, the ocean's inner soul is uncovered. Cloudy water, now several feet from the mean, reveals the existence of an apathetic society. The pristine habitat of six hours earlier is gone. Now there are aluminum cans, plastic wrappers, syringes, and unsightly blobs of tar we always called tanker turds.

I wondered how many houses were purchased at high tide, by owners who found out that at low tide it was impossible to get a boat in or out to the dock.

I wanted to live life at high tide.

The first house the realtor showed me was in Key West. It sat at the end of a large, nice canal. The only problem with the canal was that it was stagnant. There was not enough tidal flow to clear up the water.

"Don't you even want to look at the house, sir?" the salesman asked

"No, I don't think so. The water is most important to me. I can work on or rebuild a house. I can't improve on the condition of the waterfront."

The fourth home we viewed was for me. The smell of low tide still remained in the air. It was August 14 and the temperature was in the nineties. The scent of rotting sargassum weed was a fragrance that was capable of recalling past memories and feelings. It's funny how certain smells can do that. For a moment I found myself in a different time and place. It was refreshing. Although everything was perfect about this particular home and location, I didn't act too interested.

"What's that awful smell?" I asked.

"I'm not really sure," the realtor replied. "It seems to be everywhere down here though. It's worse at different times of the day."

The house was nice and neat, nothing fancy. With about two

thousand square feet on one floor, it was just right. With a large Florida room and bedroom facing the water, it had french doors that opened out onto a large cement deck. There was a small, well landscaped yard with plenty of tall palm trees. Another plus was that it was located on Cudjoe Key, only a couple of blocks from Coco's Cantina. Since Limbo first introduced me to Coco's, I had become a regular. Carlos and Flora were now almost family. They kinda looked out for me. If I didn't show up for a day or two they would call or check on me. They were not only great cooks, they were now great friends. Whenever I would show up for supper, Denise or Flora would always get me a cold Corona with a lime, and go push A6 on the jukebox. I'd sip my brew and listen to Jimmy singing "Living and Dying in 3/4 Time," while Carlos was frying up the day's catch. It never mattered what it was—grouper, dolphin, yellowtail, or mangrove snapper—it always was cooked to perfection. Being located near Coco's Cantina definitely was not reason enough for me to spend all my savings on a home. But it didn't hurt either.

After a full day of real estate shopping, the realtor and I returned to his office on Sugarloaf.

"Those are the best buys in the Keys at the moment, Mr. Taylor. Did you decide on which house fits your needs?" he asked.

I told him I wasn't too impressed with any of his choices and asked him to let me think about it. I told him I had a friend up in Marathon who was in real estate. I laid it on pretty thick. I was not interested, the prices were too high and the locations were all wrong. These were a few strategies I'd picked up from Charles, Sr.

"Well, I guess if I had to pick one, that house on Cudjoe might do," I said. I really liked it better than anything I had seen in the Keys. After pointing out all of its bad features I offered him thirty percent less than it was listed for.

"I'm sure the owner would not even entertain that offer, Mr. Taylor. It's much too low," he said.

I told him to please write up a contract with the proposal or I'd see what my friend in Marathon had to offer. I signed the proposal and left.

I was only five minutes from Limbo's, but by the time I got back, he was already on the phone with my realtor.

"Here, Powell, the phone's for you," Limbo said.

"You did it, Powell. You fooled me big time. I can't believe it, but the owner took your offer. He said he needs to close in the next couple of days," Mr. Realtor said. "If I'd known he would sell for that price, I'd have bought it myself."

The Realtor explained to me that the owner of the house made his living in ways that were somewhat frowned upon by our society. His latest venture found him out of fuel, after a long chase by the Marine Patrol. He was arrested right there in Cudjoe Bay with a large boat full of the "evil weed."

"If he is to stay out of prison, he has to pay his attorney by the end of the week. The deal is only good if you close by this Thursday," he said.

I agreed, and Mr. Smiles, the realtor, said he would set it all up.

After showing the house to Limbo, he gave me his blessing and said, "You did good, Powell." We feasted at Coco's and told them my good news.

Chapter Nine

Limbo and I both agreed on one important point. If he and I were to split the more than generous reward, we would have to solve this case without anyone's help. I knew it would be much more dangerous without Customs or the sheriff's office backing us up. But, when I'd think of that million, the dangers would subside. I spent weeks surveying the situation at work trying not to be too obvious. Most information came from Jenny and the jewelers in the back. I nosed around the accounting department asking a few questions.

While I was playing detective at work, Limbo was checking into a few things himself. He made a visit to the grieving widow and quickly found out she didn't like her new life. She said she was forced into the inheritance business and regretted it. She told Limbo she would rather have her husband back than his ten million dollars. She was a bitter woman and she convinced Limbo that Winston Sloan and Harrison Gray were responsible for her husband's death. He assured her that we would look into his disappearance and find out exactly what occurred on that fishing trip in the Bahamas.

After much thought, Limbo and I decided to take different courses. He would investigate and pry into Harrison Gray's life and learn the when, why and how about his every move. I would do the same with my boss, Mr. Winston Sloan.

Over the next five weeks we learned more than we had expected. The two men were certainly involved in something.

On one Thursday afternoon, an older couple entered the jewelry store and asked me if they could see *The Reef*. I had been informed on more than one occasion that when this happened I was to summon Mr. Sloan.

"Excuse me, sir, let me get Mr. Sloan to show you this beautiful piece of art. He is much more familiar with it than I am," I said. "And anyway, he can describe it better than I can."

I stood out of sight, but within hearing distance. The lady was dressed as if she was on her way to the opera. Her low cut gown accentuated the strand of South Seas pearls around her slender neck. She wore a matching bracelet and earrings. I guessed the set to cost somewhere in the two-to- three-hundred thousand range.

The pink luster of the pearls was complemented by the bright auburn shade of her shoulder length hair. At about thirty-five years, she was a tall, slender, long-legged beauty with no color. Although her bare legs and arms were too pale for my taste, they did not distract from the elegance of the high-priced pearls she so fashionably wore draped across her white breasts, wrist and ear lobes.

When Mr. Sloan brought out *The Reef*, they were both quite impressed. They agreed that it was the most beautiful work of its kind they had ever seen. However the lady thought she would rather put the money in a large diamond ring. After a rather loud argument with her husband, she said, "Oh, I don't care Harry, get the damn thing if you like. I don't know why you even brought me in here. You already had your mind made up before you ever saw it." I then heard something that just about made me choke. Mr. Sloan said to the couple. "At seven hundred fifty thousand dollars, it's really a bargain."

The lady and I could not believe our ears.

"Harry, you must be out of your fucking mind," the lady said as she stormed out, leaving her husband at the counter.

The man told Mr. Sloan he would take it as he was writing out his check. I was not believing my ears. I knew this piece was worth one hundred ninety-five thousand dollars tops. Why in the world would Harry pay three quarters of a million dollars for it?

Mr. Sloan told Harry that he needed the name and address of his wife and a recent photo of her for the appraisal. I was just wondering what in the hell he needed a photo of the lady for, when I sneezed. I walked out and past the two, trying not to look too suspicious. I heard Mr. Sloan say, "I would like a photo of your wife just to keep on file with the appraisal." I like to remember who buys my better pieces of jewelry. I can always look up the appraisal and know the owner's face from their photo."

It sounded a little weird to me at the time. Mr. Sloan then took Harry in the back room out of my sight.

I asked Jenny if she remembered who purchased *The Reef* before. I got the impression Jenny was not particularly happy with my request. However, she went over to the computer, pecked away at the keys and said, "Here it is, Doctor and Mrs. Frank Davidson. They bought it on January 10, and Dr. Davidson returned it on the 20th."

Jenny told me she never knew exactly why he returned it but that she really didn't understand why they bought it in the first place. After a little prying on my part she told me the Davidsons didn't seem to belong together. They argued the entire time they were in the store. Another interesting point Jenny made was that Dr. Davidson was fifty years old and his bride was about eighty. She thought they made quite an odd couple.

I looked over her shoulder and memorized Dr. Davidson's address on Big Coppitt Key. Later I would write it all down in my notes, so I could compare with Limbo's findings.

"Why do you want to know all this, Powell?" Jenny asked.

"Oh, I'm just curious."

I grabbed some scratch paper and jotted down everything I could remember about both the new and old buyers of *The Reef*. I wasn't sure why, but I was positive this gold treasure was somehow responsible for Mr. Sloan's partner's disappearance. I had a theory but was almost too scared to believe it. I didn't want to even think

I was right until I could talk to Limbo and find out what he had learned from the widow.

It startled me when Jenny came up behind me and asked if I heard about the hurricane that had popped up off west Africa. It was now one hundred fifty miles east of Miami with ninety-five mile per hour winds.

"No, I haven't heard about it," I replied. "I've been too busy moving into my new home and getting settled in to watch the tube or read the newspaper."

"Well, Powell, it doesn't look good. They're forecasting it could hit the Keys in less than ninety-two hours,"Jenny said.

I had never been in the direct path of a hurricane. The threat of a hurricane hitting didn't really intimidate me like I guessed it did Jenny.

"Do you want to come over to my house for a hurricane party in a couple of days?" I asked. "You can bring Hemingway and we'll grill some dolphin up and have a few brews."

"Powell, this is not something to take lightly. A level-five hurricane can easily wipe out Key West and everything on it." She said, "Never mind, Powell. You're impossible!"

I was sure having a hard time convincing Jenny what a nice person I was. I decided to worry about that and the hurricane later. I needed to stay focused on my million dollar mission.

Between my job at the jewelry store, trying to settle into my new abode, solve murders, and get lucky with Jenny, I was beginning to fray around the edges. I needed to go fishing soon.

After work, I went by and talked Jeffrey out of a cup of con leche. He was as much of an addict to Cuban coffee as I was and had a coffee machine set up in the kitchen of The Saltwater Angler. After talking fishing and unwinding a bit, I returned to my home at mm 22.5. Although it was close to eleven, Limbo was inside waiting on me. He was the only other person with a key to my new place. I tried to give Jenny one, but she cussed me and called me names.

Limbo and I had a mountain of evidence to go over. We spent hours reviewing what we had learned. I went first.

"Limbo, something is definitely strange about the goings on at Caribbean Jewelry," I said.

I explained about the couple buying *The Reef* for seven hundred fifty thousand dollars. I told him the name and address of the first buyers that I so cleverly picked off the computer when Jenny had punched it up.

"Frank Davidson?" Limbo screamed. "You've got to be kidding!"

"No, Limbo I'm not, that's their name. Doctor and Mrs. Frank Davidson," I replied. "Do you know them, and do they still live on Big Coppitt?"

Limbo looked puzzled as he said, "Yeah, I've heard of them, but THEY don't live on Big Coppitt anywhere, just he does.

"You see, the Mrs. is quite dead. I know because Customs was working with the FBI on that case. It was some kind of fish poisoning, if I remember. They said it was a bizarre rarity in this area."

When I heard that, I decided to tell Limbo my theory about what I felt was happening in this little paradise.

I started my story with the mysterious return of *The Reef* after Dr. Davidson purchased it for his wife.

"There was no record of a credit or any money returned to the doctor. He paid seven hundred fifty thousand dollars for a piece of art that was worth one hundred ninety-five thousand dollars, and when he returned it, he didn't get a dime back," I said.

"That makes no sense at all, Powell, maybe you're mistaken," Limbo said.

I assured him I was not. It took me another hour or so to explain.

"Here's the way I see it Limbo. I don't know how it ever got started, but the word has circulated somehow. I truly think Harrison Gray is a hit man. He works for Sloan and is much too wealthy for his position at the store. He hardly ever works and then it's only after hours. He's really secretive. Jenny told me he has a huge place on the Atlantic, a sixty-foot Hatteras and a seaplane. She thinks he only started working for Sloan less than a year ago and when he arrived he had nothing to his name."

Limbo told me that I certainly made sense. He said he could attest to Jenny's story.

"I'll tell you all about Mr. Gray when you finish," Limbo said.

"He was also on the fishing trip with Sloan and the partner that slipped off the face of the earth," I continued. "I believe *The Reef* is a deadly decoy, used to kill off loving spouses. The thought of losing an expensive divorce battle or maybe not collecting a life insurance policy is reason enough to exterminate your not so loved one.

"I think Harrison Gray killed Sloan's partner in the Bahamas and somehow poisoned Mrs. Davidson. He's probably planning the demise of poor ol' Harry's wife as we talk."

"Who's Harry?" Limbo interrupted.

I explained all about the episode with Harry and his wife and yet another purchase of *The Reef.* I had Limbo's strict attention as I continued. "This is what has to be happening. Someone decides, for whatever reasons, that it would be more profitable or advantageous to kill off their spouse. They come into Caribbean Jewelry Co. and talk to Winston Sloan. Winston charges them seven hundred fifty thousand dollars for *The Reef* and a murder. Mr. Sloan has an appraisal typed up in the victim's name along with their photo. He then gives this information to the head of security, Mr. Gray. Next we're reading in the paper about some outlandish accident that occurred, leaving a grieving husband or wife. *The Reef* then shows back up in the store, awaiting its next assignment.

"The customer tells the employees at the jewelry store that he had purchased it for his lovely wife. Now that she has had a terrible accident he just couldn't bear the thought of having it in the house. Of course he never gets his three quarters of a million dollars back. Nice little front. Nice and neat," I said.

Limbo was mesmerized. The only thing that was still a puzzle was how the people found Sloan.

"Powell, there's no telling how many murders these guys have committed. Do you think Sloan's partner found out about this scam and confronted him with it in the Bahamas?" Limbo said, thinking out loud.

He continued to tell me everything I had feared to be true about Harrison Gray.

The good thing about Limbo's connections with Customs was his access to their computers. He could check anyone's background.

Harrison Gray came to Key West three years ago, from Chicago. He ran security for a large auto dealer there. Although never proven, it was rumored that the car dealer was backed with underground monies. Gray lived the same lavish lifestyle in Chicago that he now enjoyed in Key West.

Harrison Gray had never married. He was a loner and apparently did not make friends, either in Chicago or Key West. If he did have friends, Limbo couldn't find them.

Limbo thought of something and ran out to his car. When he returned, he had a folder in his arms.

"Just what I thought!" Limbo said as he paged through the file.

He showed me a picture of an older woman lying lifeless on a morgue gurney with a white sheet at her neck. It was a cold and unfeeling photo.

Mrs. Davidson died of ciguatera poisoning, on the fourteenth of January," Limbo said.

That coincides exactly with my theory, Limbo," I answered. "Let's see here, where is it? Yeah, here it is. Dr. Davidson bought *The Reef* on January tenth and returned it on the twentieth. It fits, Limbo."

By the end of the evening we were both convinced that Caribbean Jewelry Co. was manufacturing murder, not jewelry.

I was really interested in what had happened in the Bahamas and Limbo wanted to investigate Mrs. Davidson's demise. We agreed that for the next couple of days I would look into the disappearance of Sloan's partner, while Limbo researched fish poisoning. We had to be certain we were on the right course before we made any accusations or confronted Sloan.

It was well after midnight. Limbo decided to stay the night, rather than to drive the few miles to Summerland.

The next morning I was up before the sun; Limbo had already left. I figured he was probably taking his morning swim. Again, I smiled as I found myself saying aloud, "He ain't right."

Before work, I ran by Jenny's house to make peace. I wasn't sure if she was really worth all this trouble, however, Dawn was still living four hundred miles away.

Earlier in the week I had stopped by the "Cat House" off Duval

Street and bought Hemingway a little catnip toy. I was saving it for the right moment. I felt today was it.

When Jenny opened the door, she was still in her nightgown. For some reason she looked sad. I also thought it odd that she was not dressed. She had to be at work in twenty minutes, the same as I did.

"Here, Jenny, I brought Hemingway a little mouse to play with." I was about to tell her it was a peace offering, when she burst into tears and slammed the door in my face.

"What the hell is her problem?" I thought. All the way to work I cussed all women and blamed them for every problem this world has. Limbo was right when he said, "If they didn't have that thing between their legs, there'd be a bounty on them."

When I arrived at work, Mr. Sloan and Harrison Gray were in deep conversation. They never saw me as I passed by the open door to Sloan's office.

I was certain they were discussing the best way to rid Harry of his troubles. I was close enough to peep through the crack of the door and to see the appraisal papers complete with the photo of Mrs. Harry.

I was positive I would learn the full story when the phone rang. I jumped back about two feet, scampered around the corner to the sales floor and answered, with a slight quiver in my voice, "Caribbean Jewelry Co., can I help you?"

Sloan and Gray came out of the office and seemed surprised to see me.

"Who is it?" Sloan asked.

"It's Jenny, sir. She's sick and won't make it in today," I replied.

The two turned and returned to Sloan's office. This time they closed the door behind them.

Jenny had apologized for the way she had acted earlier. Between the sobbing and crying she explained why she was so upset. Although her story was a sad one, I had a terrible time keeping a straight face.

Jenny had accidentally killed her favorite feline. Hemingway, her cat, used up all of his nine lives in less than thirty minutes.

"Powell, if you ever kid me about this I swear I'll never talk to you again," Jenny said as she told her sorrowful tale.

Jenny was doing her laundry. She had just fed Hemingway and was transferring her wash to the dryer. She went to the kitchen and got her tennis shoes out of the sink, where she had washed them by hand. After throwing the shoes in the dryer with the wet clothes she turned it on. The shoes would make such a racket as they spun around she closed the door to the laundry room. When she returned half an hour later, she found more than dry clothes. When she opened the door to the dryer, poor ol' Hemingway fell out. Besides being stiff as a board he was half cooked.

I know it had to be an awful and traumatic episode for Jenny, but somehow I found it a little humorous. It's possible she was right. Maybe I was obscene. I had an uncontrollable urge to ask her if her pussy was fluffy or if she used a fabric softener. Instead, I was sympathetic and assured her that he probably went into shock right away and didn't feel any pain. It sounded fairly reasonable and she bought it.

"Thanks Powell, that makes me feel a little better," she said.

After hanging up I wondered how long it would take to get all of the cat hair out of her underwear. I am a sick person and not funny at all. I wondered if I could get my money back for the catnipped rat?

When Sloan heard that I was off the phone, he came up to me and said, "We're closing early, Powell, you can go home now."

"Why?" I answered.

"Powell, don't you watch TV or look at the newspapers? We have a huge storm bearing down on us. It's serious. It's a hurricane. Get some candles, batteries, ice and any other supplies you may need and board up your house. We'll see you after it blows through."

"Yes, sir," I said.

As I was driving home that afternoon, I noticed the sky was a strange tint of grey. An eerie aura filled the air. The roads were all but abandoned. People were busy nailing plywood over windows and doors. Others were tying down grills, cookers and lawn furniture. I managed to get an AM station on the radio and the weather report was not looking good. I sensed fear in the woman's voice. U.S. 1 was a disaster of its own, with thousands of tourists and locals all trying to leave paradise at the same time.

It was too late for me to evacuate. Far worse than riding out a category five hurricane in your home would be trying it in your automobile.

Final preparations throughout the lower Keys found people flocking to supermarkets for last-minute supplies. I decided to wait until the stores weren't so packed. I figured in a couple of hours I could run up to the Mini-Market on Summerland and get all I needed.

As I turned the corner to my house, a special weather update was broadcast live from the National Hurricane Center in Miami. The storm had strengthened considerably. With winds of one hundred seventy-two miles per hour and a central pressure of nine hundred sixteen millibars, the storm was expected to worsen by landfall. From the estimates they were giving, Hurricane Agnes should hit land somewhere between West Palm Beach and south of Miami Beach by seven o'clock tomorrow morning. We should begin to see winds in the seventy-five to eighty-mile per hour category by midnight. The tides were expected to surge to fifteen to twenty feet where the eye of Agnes crossed land.

I was beginning to get a little worried. Maybe I should have taken this storm stuff a little more seriously. I was listening so intently to the radio as I turned in the drive that I didn't notice right away that the windows on my new home were already boarded over. Limbo banged on my car window and asked if I was going to ride the storm out in my car or what? I was glad to see him.

"Come on Powell, we've got a lot to do," he said. "Go inside and fill up your bathtubs and sinks with water. I'll tie down your boat and secure the stuff outside."

"What's with the water in the bathtubs?" I asked.

"Don't argue, Powell, we don't have time. Just get moving."

Limbo helped me for a couple more hours until he felt I was ready for Agnes. He couldn't believe that I hadn't been to the store for supplies. He made me a list and said, "Get your ass up there and hurry back. This could be the worst storm Florida has ever seen."

Some of the items on the "Limbo list" included batteries, bottled water, candles, matches, canned foods, plenty of ice, first aid items, and a transistor radio.

On the way to the store I wondered if they still made transistor radios.

I had to park a half mile away from the supermarket on the opposite side of the highway. It was a mad house. Unfortunately, I wasn't the only dumb ass to wait till the last minute. People were yelling, cussing and fighting over everything. Each register had a long line of twenty or so irate customers. The most popular items being grabbed seemed to be beer, ice and batteries. Although the owners of the mini-mart seemed very irritated, they had to be happy. This storm would totally deplete their inventory. A near sell out would have to excite them. But then I thought about it. The big blow was less than twenty hours away and they were still at work. Who secured their homes? Who boarded their windows and brought in their lawn furniture? I heard a crash and glanced outside. A new Mercedes had just smashed into the side of a pickup. Neither driver payed any attention to it. They continued on their way. I wondered if any of the three people parked in the handicapped zones were indeed disabled. It would be sad if someone who truly needed that space had to park so far away because of three impatient jerks. The winds were beginning to gust.

After completing Limbo's list I grabbed a family-sized bucket of fried chicken and returned to Cudjoe.

Sensing my anxiety, Limbo decided to wait out the storm at my house. He assured me he had already secured his place and it was storm-proof. I didn't argue with his decision.

We put batteries in the radio, and put candles and matches where we could find them. For the moment, we still had electricity and telephones. The weather channel kept us informed as Agnes set her course for south Florida. I asked Limbo what happened in the days before weather satellites, The National Weather Service and television.

He said usually it was disastrous. In the old days, by the time you felt the directions of the winds suddenly change, or a steady drop of the barometer, it was too late. Many people died in hurricanes because they didn't have the information we now get well in advance.

I called Jenny's house, but there was no answer. She was probably in Idaho by now. She was possibly a great deal more sane than I gave her credit for. Maybe I should have left town. It's too late now, I thought.

One of the most depressing things about a hurricane is the waiting. The news media is comparing this storm to every other hurricane that has hit the United States in the last century. Death counts are given for each of the past storms.

By nightfall, the winds and seas had increased with amazing suddenness. The severity of a storm is magnified by the absence of light. We lost power about four o'clock in the morning. The last thing I heard was that Agnes was expected to cross the Florida Keys between Islamorada and the Tortugas. Winds were more than one hundred eighty-five miles per hour and were sure to destroy most anything in its path. About ninety percent of the Keys had been successfully evacuated. The rest of us dummies were at the mercy of Agnes.

Limbo and I tried to talk about Sloan, Gray, the widow and Dr. Davidson, but somehow couldn't keep focused. We decided to get on it one hundred percent after the storm passed.

The wind howled. Palm fronds went airborne, hitting the side of the house too often for comfort. Being caught in the heart of a hurricane was certainly no party. I stood at my front door, watching as street lights, utility poles and trees littered the streets.

Daylight did not ease my fears. Uprooted palm trees were across power lines and floating in the canal behind the house. Capsized boats of all kinds were drifting by with the fast falling tides. The eye of the storm passed over in about thirty minutes. The back side of Agnes brought winds from the opposite direction. Thankfully, they were not as severe. We found out later that the eye had crossed directly over Islamorada and spared the lower Keys from total devastation. For the next five days I learned a great deal about cleaning up a hurricane's aftermath. Limbo and I were lucky. Our homes and boats were pretty much untouched. We removed trees, docks and all the litter from our yards the first day following Agnes. We then helped our neighbors with their clean-up tasks. There is nothing like a good disaster to bring friends and neighbors to each others sides to help out. I soon learned the importance of saving water in the tubs and sinks. The main water supply into the Keys was severely damaged east of Islamorada and we had no piped water for five days. No water meant no showers, no drinking water from the tap, and, worst of all, no toilet flushing.

We had to take water from the tub and pour it in the back of the commode for a flush. A storm like Agnes makes you appreciate all of the little things we take for granted. On the sixth day, our running water returned. A day later, our electricity. Paradise was beginning to get back to normal. Governor Askew declared the upper Keys a natural disaster. The Red Cross, the National Guard and insurance adjusters jammed U.S. 1.

It turned out we were lucky. The storm had lost some speed just before landfall. Although still packing winds of one hundred forty-five miles per hour, it could have been a lot worse.

One of the local Miami TV stations had set up in Marathon to broadcast live updates in the hurricane's wake. It was good to have television. I was in touch with the world again.

During the six o'clock news report on the Friday after the electricity returned, I saw something that made my head spin and turned my stomach. I ran to the phone and called Limbo.

"Turn on channel six, Limbo. Hurry!"

It was not the total death toll that made me ill. In fact, as most hurricanes go, this one was kind. Four people in the upper Keys lost their lives and only one in Key West.

"That's pretty good statistics for a hurricane the size of Agnes," Limbo stated.

"No, Limbo, I didn't mean how many. Look at the name of the woman who died in Key West," I said.

"Yeah, Powell, her name was Agnes, the same as the hurricane. Kinda funny, huh?" he replied.

They kept showing photos of Agnes and her husband. I finally realized why Limbo didn't know what the hell I was talking about. He hadn't ever seen them.

"That's him Limbo!" I yelled. "Agnes' husband, that's Harry. That's the Harry that bought *The Reef* from Sloan ten days ago. Now his wife is dead from an accident. You bet your ass we're on the right track here."

"I'm on my way over, Powell, see you in a minute," Limbo said, and he hung up.

He arrived in record time. He was able to cut the ten-minute trip from Summerland to Cudjoe in half. He was scribbling in his notebook as he came in.

"Let's see now, Powell," Limbo said without looking up. "What do we have here exactly? We're pretty sure Sloan is setting up murders. Harrison Gray is probably the hit man, and Sloan's partner found out about his sideline and is now floating face down in the Bahamas. Besides his partner, we suspect him of killing Mrs. Frank Davidson and now Harry's Agnes. If we're going to collect our more than generous fee from Sloan's partner's wealthy widow, we'll have to get a little more evidence."

"Limbo, we also know for a fact that *The Reef* is a masquerade for murder," I added.

We agreed that the next day we would earn our million. The remaining hurricane clean-up could be postponed.

Limbo wanted to talk to the widow once again and feel her out. He also was going to try to collect some expense monies. Afterwards, he would drop by to see Dr. Davidson and then Harry.

I decided to go fishing in the Bahamas. I called down to Key West. A pleasant feminine voice on the other end said, "Good evening, the Saltwater Angler."

"Can I please speak with Jeffrey?" I asked.

"Jeffrey, this is Powell, you wanna go fishing in the Bahamas this weekend? I thought, since you just got your pilot's license and that new Cessna, you might want to fly down to Deep Water Cay and catch a few bonefish."

Although Jeffrey hadn't a clue about why I really wanted to visit the Bahamas, he was more than eager. I agreed to pay all expenses if he flew his plane. I thought it might be too easy to trace my whereabouts if I flew commercially.

"Sounds like a great adventure. Sure, I'll go," Jeffrey replied.

Chapter Ten——

The weather had cleared enough by mid-morning for us to depart
Key West Airport. Jeffrey was a beginning pilot who not yet had
his instrument rating. That worked well with me, because I was not
fond of flying around in the clouds for extended periods of time.
Jeffrey's plane was spotless. He took pride in it and it showed. It
was a Cessna 180 Tail Dragger. What that means, I found out on
that trip, is that the wheel is in the rear of the plane. It had high
wings which made the thirty-minute flight over to Deep Water
great.

Jeffrey's Cessna, with twelve-inch lettering on the tail that
read N55214, was bright white with red trim. A comfortable
airplane with room for four people, Cessna N55214 was a joy to
travel in. However, on this flight to the Bahamas, there was room
only for two. Baggage, rod tubes, tackle and assorted fishing gear
filled the two rear seats. I believe Jeffrey was unhappy with the
clutter. His pride and joy was untidy.

Jeffrey was cautious and precise as he went through his
preflight checklist, a procedure I felt good about. Even the most

seasoned pilots should mimic Jeffrey's moves. We can all have memory lapses at times.

Miami's tower flew us V. F. R. at forty-five hundred feet up to Ft. Lauderdale and across to Freeport, Bahamas. We landed in Freeport to clear customs. When we cleared the runway and began to taxi toward the main terminal, I noticed we had entered a relaxed environment. There were no jet ways, no monorails, no shuttles and no baggage carts. The islands are a comfort zone, a place to unwind, loosen up and rest. The Bahamian welcome mat was a greeting of pleasure and enjoyment. For the next few days I would have to force myself to remember why I was here. It would be tempting to slip into the tourist mode that this vacation paradise readily makes available.

Jeffrey and I deplaned, locked up the Cessna and entered the tropically decorated terminal. The entrance was beautifully landscaped with palms, yuccas and bright pink flowery hibiscus trees. The interior walls of the airport were painted with vivid colors depicting an underwater world with tropical fish, lobster and turtles.

"Please follow de yella line."

Following the instructions of the voice over the intercom, Jeffrey and I found our way back to the Customs booth. The two men behind the counter were friendly and efficient. They both wore neatly ironed tan uniforms with green trim and colorful patches on each arm. Both were Bahamian. One man was light-skinned, the other much darker. One checked our passports as the other started to inspect our luggage. But, then they saw our fly rods and passed us through.

"Going to do a bit of fishing, mon?" the dark skinned man asked.

"Yes, sir, we're going to Deep Water Cay to catch some bonefish," I said.

"Tell Walter I say hello and to be treating you proper during your holiday," he continued. "Good day, mon."

We hurried back to the plane, carefully loaded our baggage and began our taxi to the run-up area. Jeffrey spun the airplane around so that the propeller was facing into the wind. I found out later that the reason Jeffrey pointed the nose into the wind was to improve engine cooling. Again, Jeffrey carefully followed his written pre-takeoff checklist. Once we were ready for takeoff, we taxied onto the runway and lined up with the wide white line in the center. With his right hand, Jeffrey gently forced the throttle forward. As we began our roll down the air strip, I watched the fronds of the giant palm trees quiver from the breeze our wake created. In minutes we were suspended above Freeport, floating with the clouds. For a moment the view below reminded me of a particular row of rapacity I had traveled through near Panama City Beach. On one side of the island was beautiful coral bottomed, grassy flats full of life. Directly below us was the neon lighting from one of the many casinos scattered in the city.

As soon as Freeport disappeared behind us, we flew low and could see into the clear shallow waters with no problem.

The sun was bright and the colors reflecting from below were vivid. The sun's rays penetrated the surface of the water illuminating the bottom as if being viewed through a powerful microscope. We had the best seat in the theater. The shallow water, or thin water as fishing guides call it, was a beautiful light green shade that flickered over the white coral background. As the tide rises and falls, it is these flats that are the feeding grounds that attract bonefish.

From our view in the Cessna we could see the entire world of the coral flats. A deep aqua-blue finger channel provides easy access and escape to and from the flats. Many areas are tan and brown from the patches of turtle grass growing. In this maze of channels and flats an occasional dark orange coral head pops up to grab our eye. The rising tides that shift the sand, marl and mud not only create a beautiful picture from the air but also provide a nursery ground for a zillion forms of sea life.

This is truly a magical place where the taste of salt air penetrates my veins and flows within my bloodstream. It was unfortunate that on this trip I would not be able to completely enjoy this mystical environment. I had an important task to accomplish I needed to pay attention and remain focussed. Limbo, the widow and my bank account all depended on it.

Suddenly, Jeffrey said, "Look at the size of that bonefish, Powell!" As he laughingly pointed to a nurse shark crossing the flats.

Jeffrey and I discussed things such as fly fishing, the Marquesas, Fantasy Fest, women, gays, kids, old people, Cubans, guiding, tarpon, music, airplanes, sunken treasures, Lotto, pirates and even politics. We did not discuss Sloan, murder or other types of violence. It was a pleasant flight. We knew each other a little better by the time we saw the three thousand-foot runway at the Deep Water Cay Resort. After a perfect landing, the plane came to a stop at the end of the runway. We were only a few feet from the crystal clear water that the Bahamas are famous for. Waiting there by the water were two of the local guides in a golf cart.

"Hallo, Mr. Jeff and Mr. Powell, we glad you here," one of them said.

"It's good to be here," Jeffrey replied.

After securing the plane we loaded our bags and tackle, jumped on the back of the cart and went to our room. Our room was at the opposite end of the island in the "Drake Cottage" named after the first owner of the club, Gil Drake, Sr. who had since sold it.

"The bar open 'round five, an' dinnah be served at six, mon," we were told.

We unpacked, took a swim, walked the flats and returned to the bar at precisely five fifteen. I was hoping to get a conversation going with someone who remembered Sloan and his partner's fatal fishing trip.

I was disappointed to see the bar was empty when we arrived. The more I talked to the bartender the more I realized that she probably knew more about the comings and goings of clients than anyone at the club. I was definitely not mistaken. Voiletta, the club bartender was born in MacCleans Town just across the channel from Deep Water Cay. She was a lovely lady who more than thirty years ago, helped crush rock for the first lodge. Later she became a maid, then a cook and finally a bartender. That evening I learned a great deal about Voiletta. She had two grown, adopted children, Ann and Tell, five grandchildren and a well-fed hog named "Me One."

"I luv de work here at Deep Water. I meet de very nice people. I sometime meet more interesting peoples den others," she told us.

Jeffrey took his cold beer and walked out to the ocean. I saw a window of opportunity and asked Voiletta, "Do you remember some guys from Key West who were down here fishing last year? There were three of them, one was named Sloan, and one was Harrison Gray," I said.

"Ah yes, mon, I remember dem well. Dose three men had fished here many times before, but it be de lady's first time visitin'," Voiletta said with a huge white grin.

"What lady?" I asked.

"Look here, mon," she said as she pointed to a picture on the wall behind the bar. I went around the bar and got close enough to see who was holding up the eight-pound bonefish. It was Sloan's partner and his grieving widow. "Well I'll be damned," I thought.

I was pretty shocked to see her. It's funny, she never mentioned that she was here with her husband when he died.

"It really was too baad 'bout her husban', I mean dat way he die out dere swimmin' an' all. Walta, he never get over it to dis day,"said Voiletta.

After about ten beers and a thousand questions I had a better idea of what exactly happened out there. Walta, or rather Walter, was one of the guides Sloan always used on his trips. Since one of Voiletta's many duties included matching up anglers with guides, I requested to fish tomorrow with "Walta." I then asked about the telephone service only to find out there was none.

"Da closest phone be in MacCleans Town," I was told. I wished I could get ahold of Limbo before he faced the mysterious lady in the photo I was staring at. I didn't necessarily want him to question her about it, just be careful with her. Hopefully, he would collect a few thousand dollars for expenses while I was gone. I'd have to think a little harder about why she was here and what it all meant. I staggered to the dining room, met up with Jeffrey and had a delightful meal of baked grouper and conch fritters. The next morning, Jeffrey and I were at the docks early waiting for Walter. He and five other guides came by boat each morning from MacCleans Town. They arrived about six-thirty. Walter was a local "fellah" who had been guiding at Deep Water for nearly twenty years. A man of few words, Walter was very dark-skinned, wore long khaki pants, dark sunglasses, a white long-sleeve shirt with Deep Water Cay embroidered over the pocket and a faded baseball cap. After loading Walter's skiff, he ran us through a long network of channels and canals before finally entering the ocean.

Walter killed the engine and from the gunwale began poling us toward an area that seemed abundant in bird life.

"Da birds be tellin' me dat der be plenty of bait on dat flat up ahead. De bones be eatin' da same ting as da birds," Walter said as he quit poling the boat forward.

After a short lesson on casting and fly presentation to bonefish, Walter compared his skiff to a clock.

"Straight ahead be twelve o'clock and de engine be at six," he said pointing behind us.

Jeffrey and I were familiar with this technique but let Walter explain it just the same. Walter's boat was made in the Bahamas and seemed perfect for these shallow waters. Like my Maverick and Limbo's Hewes, Walter's boat could float in about eight inches of water. It was a very stable boat. The three of us could stand on the same gunwale and the skiff barely leaned in that direction. The interior of the boat was wide open with no obstacles. There was very little that could tangle our fly lines. Walter finished teaching his lesson and began moving our skiff toward the flat filled with birds.

We took turns on the bow casting to and catching bonefish. The weather was perfect and Walter was a fine guide.

"Bonefish, ten 'clock, sixty feet, mon!" Walter would say in a loud whisper.

We would spot the fish before casting to them. By lunch time we'd both caught and released four bones each.

When it's time to eat, all of the Deep Water guides meet up at "Lunch Beach." They beach their skiffs and leave their guests to enjoy lunch and each others company. The guides walk down a hundred yards or so under some shade trees. "Lunch Beach" is probably fifteen or twenty miles from civilization and is a peaceful, sandy sanctuary. While the fishermen discussed who caught what and which guides did this or that, I bet Walta and the rest of the guides did the same, discussing dis an dat.

Jeffrey said, "I'll bet they're over there under that big tree talking about us spoiled tourists. They're probably saying something like, "Hey, mon, I poled dat fat ass mon all day long and jes when I git him to de bonefish he can't cast but ten feet. I want to throw him off de boat when he say to me it be my fault he miss de fish."

We were fairly sure we were right. Every so often the whole bunch of them would burst into laughter. We knew, however, Walta would most definitely tell them how professional Jeffrey and I were. We smiled.

Before the afternoon fishing began, I got Walter to the side, away from Jeffrey's ears. I asked him if he would meet me in the bar after supper to tie some flies. I didn't really want to tie flies and maybe he sensed that. Although a bit hesitant, he finally agreed.

"I be der 'bout eight, Powell," Walter said.

The remainder of the day was just as pleasant as the morning had been. Jeffrey asked Walter what they talked about during lunch.

"Do ya'll talk about us foreigners coming over here taking advantage of your hospitality, food, fishing and letting you pole our sorry asses around these beautiful flats all day? Do you call us a bunch of spoiled pussies and tell each other about all of our fuck ups that day?" Jeffrey asked.

Walter just smiled a huge toothy grin and said, "No mon, we never would think dat."

We all three then had a good laugh. From that moment Walter was a little more at ease with us.

We talked Walter into picking up a rod, stepping to the bow, and trying his luck. Jeffrey poled the boat as I watched Walter cast. He was an extraordinary angler. One of the best memories from that day occurred that afternoon while Walter was casting.

Jeffrey poled around a rocky coral point along an edge of a deep channel that tapered into water so shallow I was sure we would get stuck in the mud. Small mangrove roots were popping up like a field full of mushrooms after a good summer rain. Jeffrey was stalking a tailing bonefish. The water was so skinny that the belly of the bonefish was rubbing the coral bottom while his tail and dorsal fin sliced the surface. Using my favorite bonefish rod, Walter stripped out about seventy-five feet of fly line. With the line laying at his feet on the deck of the boat, I sensed a potential problem. Walter should have cast the entire line out on the water and then stripped it back in, carefully laying it on the deck. That eliminates tangling. However, Jeffrey had quickly moved us within casting range of the big bone not giving Walter time to clear his line. The front part of the fly line was on the bottom of the pile, coiled up like a kids slinky. Walta-Mon's haste could come back to haunt him.

Walter made one back cast and let the line fly forward. It was a perfect cast and the bonefish took the fly immediately. A very large fish, ten or eleven pounds, he started screaming through the three-inch water. Walter fought it for about ten minutes before getting him within reach. Then, just as I had feared, twenty feet from the fishes mouth, a huge knot in the fly line slapped the water leaving a small rooster tail on the flat surface. Walter tried to reel the knot through the guides and get it onto the reel before the fish made his final run. However, as soon as the knot cleared the fourth guide the fish decided to take off. The knot got caught in the tip and the eight-pound leader snapped instantly.

Jeffrey and I were cussing and yelling at the fish and trying to make Walter feel better when he grinned and whispered, "The wind knot is not my friend."

It was great. Walter maneuvered his skiff through the shallows and returned us to the lodge.

After another Caribbean feast of fried conch steaks, fish chowder and fresh conch salad, Jeffrey said he was ready to hit the bed. I was pleased, as it saved me from having to make up some bizarre excuse to stay at the bar.

"I'll be down later, Jeffrey, I'm going to tie a couple of flies for tomorrow," I said.

"Great, I'll see you in the morning," Jeffrey replied on his way out.

A few minutes before eight, Walta showed up at the back door. He opened the sliding glass door, slipped in and quickly sat down next to me at the bar. I could easily sense how uncomfortable he felt. Pointing under the counter Walter told Voiletta, "Me rum please." Clanking through an assortment of bottles she grabbed one from the back and placed it on the bar in front of Walter. It was a fifth of Mount Gay Rum.

"Dis be made in Barbados," Walter whispered.

I told Voiletta to put the rum on my tab. Walter was a little nervous talking about Sloan and the death of his partner. I got the feeling he had been coached on his answers concerning the accident.

For a man who had claimed he didn't drink, Walter sure did like his rum. After half a bottle, "Walta-Mon" was feeling pretty good. We moved out on the back deck away from Voiletta.

"Dat be some kinda mystery 'bout dose folks. I'd thought dat de woman be married to de other gentleman. I find out later she be married to de dead mon!" Walter said.

I went inside to get the photo off the wall behind the bar. Voiletta just smiled. When I showed the picture to Walter, he pointed to Sloan and said, "Him dere, dat be de mon she be smoothin' up to. I see dem out on da dock one evenin', and they be swappin' spit like dey ain't seen each other in a month." Everytime the door to the bar or restaurant opened, Walter would stop talking and glance around as if he were being watched. When the door would close he would continue. I felt this was the only chance I would get to push him a little farther. I needed to know what happened and why the widow was not telling the whole story.

"How did that man die anyway, Walter?" I asked.

"Oh, mon, it was not very pretty at all. No one but meself know what de truth be. Dey tell me if I tell anyone dey will find out and pay me a visit. I think I need to get dis off me mind, I mean, I know dere be a God an he not be happy wiff me if I be hidin' sometin'," Walter said as tears formed in his eyes. I was sure I was about to know the story. I had the fear of higher gods and almost two fifths of rum on my side.

It took about two hours and another bottle to get the complete story.

"Dey not know I be knowin' de whole ting, but I do. One evenin' real late I was 'bout to head back to MacCleans town when I notice dat de lady and dis here mon be goin' out in da skiff," he said as he pointed at Sloan in the picture. "I be figurin' dat dey were gonna go down de beach an take off dey clothes and begin to fuckin'. I mean, I deed tink dey were married an all. She bein' kinda good lookin', I decide to follow in der wake. I be sneakin' along, polin' de boat, bein' real quiet when sometin' catch me eye. It be de other skiff wiff de other two men, de now dead mon an' de mon you be callin' Gray. De two boats pull up to each other an' dey start to drinkin' an' talkin'. It ain't long an' de lady is standin' in de boat wiffout a stich of clothin'. All three men be kissing an' grabbin' her. Dey all seem pretty drunk. I be watchin' de lady's body movin' back an' forth when dis mon here pick up an oar an' hit dis mon up side de head."

Tears were flowing down Walter's face as he remembered that night. Walter, by pointing at the photo, had just told me that Harrison Gray knocked Sloan's partner unconscious with the oar and threw his body overboard. What he next told me, brought back the same feeling in my gut as when Lunker slaughtered that baby manatee.

"Dey den start de engine an' run over de mon floatin' in da water. Dey go back an' do it again an' again. I push my boat up in de mangroves an' hide till dey leave. Once dey good an' gone I take me light an' flash it in de water. De mon be sittin' on de bottom all sliced up as if a school of cuda ben feedin' on him. I reach over an' pull him in de boat. I notice he be missin' one of his legs. I be too sick feelin' to look for it by now. De water be all red from his blood an' I be wantin' to get outta dere."

Next Walter told me something that made my trip worth while. Walter had proof! Walter, being such a God-fearing man, took the body out into the mangroves near his house and buried Sloan's unfortunate partner. No one knew that Walter had done this. He promised he would never tell another soul what he just confessed to me. I convinced him to keep that promise.

Walter continued his story as if he was talking to a priest in the confessional, searching for absolution.

"De next day, all de people be runnin' round crazy here at de club. De lady tell us all dat she an' her husban' go out in de boat last night to take a swim. She say de sharks attack her husban' an' kill him an' dat she barely make it outta de water. I know she be lyin' an' most of de other guides be pretty sure too. Dey not ever know 'bout anyone get eat by sharks 'round here. Dey never say nothin' though. De lady take a few of us to de place it all happen. She start yellin' an' cryin' and pointin' in de water. She be lookin' at a Nike tennis shoe wiff a leg still attached. Well, de crabs an' shrimps be nibblin' all night on de meaty part of de flesh. By now it look just like a shark bit it off. Dey wrap it up in a towel an' we all go back to de club. Dat be de last time I ever see dose peoples. I hopes I never see dem again."

Walter was exhausted. I had an urge to tell him to say five Hail Marys, two Our Fathers and never fish with crooks again in order to cleanse his soul. I just told him "Good night and thanks" instead. I felt sure that tonight would be the first good sleep Walta might have had in many months. The next day of fishing was as enjoyable and productive as our first. Walter was happy and smiling all day. He had removed those ugly black spots from his soul, and was able to enjoy his work again. We caught twenty-two bonefish that day, a new fly fishing record at Deep Water.

As Jeffrey fished, I wrote notes so I wouldn't forget exactly how to tell Walter's story to Limbo.

When Jeffrey and I boarded his Cessna, an emotional Walter was there to bid us farewell. Besides helping the Walta-Mon rid himself of nightmares I also gave him the largest tip he had ever received since he began guiding. I promised Walter I would be back to fish again. As we rose up above the runway, I could see a teary-eyed Walter waving from below.

"That Walter is a nice guy, Powell, but he does seem a little sensitive at times," Jeffrey said.

I tried not to chuckle.

When we left Freeport, headed back to Key West, I took the notebook out of my bag. Included with my notes in the bag was a pair of binoculars, a birding book, some bonefish flies, and a new photo from behind Deep Water's bar. Although she had not a clue to its meaning, it was a farewell gift from Voiletta.

On the first page of my note pad I had scribbled down Carlos' recipe for frying fish. I had copied it months earlier when Limbo revealed Carlos' secret.

"Hey, Jeffrey, let's land at Summerland Key, pick up Limbo, and eat at Coco's Cantina," I said.

It was early enough to land, eat, and still give Jeffrey plenty of time to return to Key West before the sun disappeared.

After Jeffrey agreed, he told me he had never eaten at Coco's before.

"You're in for a treat, Jeffrey. Carlos and Flora cook the best fish in the Keys," I said.

"In fact, I just happen to have the recipe right here. You want to hear it?" I asked.

Jeffrey nodded.

"First you filet the fish—grouper, cobia or snapper work the best. My favorite is grouper. Place the filets in a pan, and squeeze fresh lime juice over them. Rub a little fresh garlic on them and sprinkle them with salt, pepper, and Sazon Completa."

"What the hell is Sazon Completa?" he said.

"It's a mixture of Cuban spices. I think it means complete seasoning."

Jeffrey informed me that he knew what it meant, he just never heard of it. I had forgotten Jeffrey's family was from Cuba, and he spoke perfect Spanish.

"You can get it at the Winn Dixie on Big Pine," I said, getting back to the recipe.

"Next, you lightly flour the filets. Then, you dip them in beaten egg and finally into medium cracker crumbs. You deep fry the filets at three hundred seventy-five degrees till they turn a golden brown color, right about the time they start to float. I can't wait."

We landed on Summerland, walked over to Limbo's house and got him to drive us to Coco's. We all three got the fried grouper.

"Hey, Carlos, the food is great as usual but you got this hot sauce a little warm." Limbo said as he dipped from the communal gallon jug to his black beans and rice.

"Hey, Limbo, you're just a big sissy," Carlos barked back.

I was glad when Jeffrey said he had to get back to Key West. I was anxious to tell Limbo what I knew and to see what he had learned. We dropped Jeffrey off at the plane, then pulled into Limbo's drive. After brewing up a huge pot of con leche, we compared stories.

I went first. I told Limbo that the widow was with them when her husband was killed. He was happy that I found a witness to the murder. After finishing my account I showed Limbo the photo with Sloan, his partner, Harrison Gray and best of all, the sad, sad widow. We agreed that the photo was a stupid mistake on their part. We also agreed to be very careful when we met with the widow from now on.

Limbo had picked up some great information himself over the long weekend. He first paid the widow a visit in order to get some spending money. We were hoping to get ten or fifteen thousand dollars up front and collect the balance of our more than generous two million after Sloan was in jail.

Sitting in her living room Limbo told the widow, "We're making some progress for you ma'am, but we could use a little money to help us out."

Limbo said she left the room and was gone for about ten minutes. He was just beginning to think that maybe he'd pissed her off or something. She returned carrying a large duffle bag that she placed in Limbo's lap.

"That ought to hold you for a while," she said. "I'll give you the balance when Sloan goes away for good."

While I was in the Bahamas questioning Walter, Limbo had done an outstanding job on the widow back in Key West. He said getting the money had been way too easy. After a quick glance in the bag, he thanked her and left.

"Powell, you might have noticed I wasn't too astonished when you told me the widow helped with her husband's murder. I had come to the same conclusion after my visit with her. There were two things that set off an alarm. The first was this. When she left the room to get the bag of loot, I noticed one of her pictures on the wall. It was a photograph of her and her husband all dressed up in formal attire toasting the camera with glasses of champagne. In the background on the coffee table was that beautiful gold sculpture, the one you had described as *The Reef*. I believe Sloan took the photo and that his partner became *The Reef's* first victim."

"That sounds right to me Limbo, but what's the second thing that clued you?" I asked.

"What do you mean, Powell?"

"You said there were two things that alarmed you— what was the other one?"

"Oh, yeah," Limbo said as he threw the duffle bag at my feet. "Look in there."

"Shit! How much is it?" I asked.

"Six hundred thousand dollars cash," he replied. "You see

what I mean, Powell? She gave us that much cash to try and convince us she was sincere. She wants to remove any guilty feelings we may have had about her. After your visit to the Bahamas, we now know for sure why she did it."

We also knew we would probably never see the balance of the money. Three hundred thousand tax-free dollars was pretty good pay for my first year in the Keys, however.

We had proof now that the widow, Gray and Sloan killed his partner. We knew how they did it and why. At least we thought it was the ten million dollar insurance policy. The reason could no longer be so Sloan and the widow could live together happily ever after. She was, in fact, trying her damnest to put him in prison for the rest of his days. She wanted her husband dead for the insurance money and Sloan wanted his partner dead for his share of the business. I could understand why she kept insisting on leaving the police out of the investigation.

As we counted out each other's three hundred thou, Limbo continued. "After I digested all the info from the widow, I paid Dr. Franklin Davidson a visit. He is a clever man. He was convincingly still mourning the death of his wife. He was careful in his responses to my questions. I told him I was a professor with the University of Miami and that I was doing research on fish poisoning. I said I had read about his wife's death in the paper. If I hadn't known better, I would have almost believed his grief was sincere. He was a good actor, but not 100 percent credible. He said the five million dollars that he collected from the insurance company meant nothing to him. He said he would rather have his wife back. I didn't buy it, Powell."

Limbo had been busy in the past couple of days. He found out that the most commonly reported fish poisoning is called ciguatera. In Florida 90 percent of all cases occur during the spring and summer months. This fit with our theory.

"How did you get all this info on fish poisoning," I asked?

"I've got a friend that works in the lab at Mariner's Hospital. He got the info from the hospital library and ran some copies off for me. The interesting part is that it's the same hospital where Dr. Davidson practices," Limbo said as he twitched his eyebrows up and down.

He thought he was quite clever. I had to agree. He sure had a lot of friends in the right places.

Limbo continued his lesson with enthusiasm. He told me, "The fish species involving ciguatera probably exceed five-hundred. The most common are grouper, red snapper, amberjack, parrot fish, triggerfish, kingfish, and Mrs. Davidson's favorite, barracuda. The fish get it by feeding on some kind of algae or protozoan dinoflagellates or some such shit. The little reef fish digest these dinoflagellates and then the larger fish feed on them."

I thought this was an interesting and clever way to kill someone. We would never be able to prove it was intentional.

Limbo told me that sixty percent of the cases reported in a Miami study followed ingestion of grouper.

I made some comments about Carlos and our meal tonight, but Limbo was too involved in his story.

He had also found out that so many reports of ciguatera followed the ingestion of barracuda that its sale is prohibited in Miami. Dr. Davidson admitted to catching and cooking the very barracuda that killed his wife. He grilled it, along with a T-bone for himself. He said his wife was a vegetarian and did not eat meat. Limbo felt this was an attempt to explain why she was the only one to eat the barracuda.

According to Dr. Davidson, his wife showed all the symptoms of ciguatera poisoning that Limbo had uncovered. About fifteen minutes after she ate the foul filet, she felt nauseous and began to vomit. She complained that her teeth were loose, and her joints ached. Next, she had diarrhea and severe abdominal pains. By the time she reached the hospital, she had chest pains, and her skull was throbbing. As the emergency team tried to diagnose the exact problem, she complained of watery eyes, tingling and numbness of the tongue and lips. Before the emergency room doctor could start the intravenous benadryl, she went into an awful seizure and stopped breathing. What a terrible way to go.

"Hey, Limbo, can you tell before you eat the fish if it's bad or not?" I asked.

"Well, that's a good question, Powell. Until recently the experts thought not. However if you research deeply enough, like I assume Dr. Davidson did, you know differently. Ciguatera is more dangerous and prevalent in larger fish. I believe that's how he did it. There's no telling how many barracuda he fed his wife, until he finally succeeded.

"He probably went fishing on the reef for large barracuda. Toothy fish such as barracuda and kingfish that are infected with ciguatera show copper-colored stains on the base of their teeth. I figure he collected a couple of these fish each time he went to the reef. He then probably threw them in a fish box. You see, the toxin can be prevented by proper refrigeration, but if you let it sit in the sun for a while it contaminates the flesh. He took those 'cuda home and cooked up the deadly meal for his unsuspecting wife. I'm sure that's how it happened, Powell, but we'll never be able to prove this one."

"That's a shame, Limbo, but I think you're right," I said.

Knowing I was wasting my time asking, I wondered if Limbo was able to get a confession out of Harry, *The Reef's* most recent beneficiary. I asked anyway.

"What about Harry and Agnes? Any proof there?"

"It's kinda the same ol' story Powell. Harry is so upset and feeling guilty about his poor Agnes' death. Although he didn't come out and tell me like Davidson did, I'm sure the seven and a half million dollars he received doesn't replace poor Agnes."

He told me that Harry and Agnes had a bitter argument before the hurricane hit. She told Harry he was a fool for buying her that golden reef. It was a waste of money and he never listened to her anymore. She supposedly took their twenty-five foot Grady White and headed to the Tortugas all alone.

"I doubt that is really what happened. I'm just as sure Harrison Gray was involved somehow," Limbo added.

They found the body floating near Garden Key only feet from the untouched Grady. They say the rough water and wind knocked her overboard. She must have hit her head on the way over and drowned as she sank to the bottom.

It was all lies, but unfortunately they were good lies. We could not prove this murder any more than we could Mrs. Davidson's. I was tired. Tomorrow I had to return to work and act as if nothing was going on. Limbo took me and my stash back to Cudjoe. I hid the money and laid my head on the pillow to study the back of my eyelids. In a few seconds, my mind went inactive, and I was fast asleep.

Chapter Eleven———

How and why does anyone get as ruthless as Sloan? He was screaming at Jennifer.

"Just do what you're told. Send him a bill anyway. He'll get what he deserves."

I was there two months earlier when Mr. Sloan promised Howard Nolan he would not bill him. Howard had purchased a diamond tennis bracelet for someone other than his wife. Not that I agree or disagree with the policy, but Sloan gave his word that he would keep it discrete and not send Mr. Nolan a bill. Howard Nolan had paid the thirty-three-percent down and charged the balance over ninety days. Winston Sloan told Mr. Nolan he would not be billed during those ninety days. Now, for some reason, Sloan decided to ruin Howard's life over an eight hundred dollar bracelet.

I sat there listening and wondering just what causes such feelings in people. Is it greed? Contempt? Revenge?

In Sloan's case I felt it was power. He liked being in control of people's lives.

I interrupted and said, "Excuse me Mr. Sloan, but I couldn't help but to overhear your conversation with Mr. Nol—"

"Don't concern yourself with it Powell. I'll handle it," was barked in my direction before I could finish my sentence.

"Fine!" I thought, "Fuck you, Sloan. I'll get your sorry ass before it's over with." I disliked Sloan more and more with each passing day. I could hardly wait for justice to heal this son of a bitch.

I was trying to suggest that I would simply phone Mr. Nolan. The moment the hint of a bill came out in our conversation, I was sure he would rush down and pay off his account. What the heck, I thought, I'll do it anyway.

Statements would be sent out in four days. I called the number on the account card. It was somewhere in the lower Keys, probably Big Pine. "Hello," a female voice answered.

I hadn't expected that.

"Is Howard in?" I said.

"No, may I help you or would you like to leave a message?"

"Um, yeah, this is Powell Taylor, could you please get Howard to give me a call." I gave her the phone number of the store, hoping she would let it drop. She didn't.

"Well, Powell, Howard will be in about five o'clock. Are you sure I can't help you? I'm Mrs. Nolan, Howard's wife.

"Umm, well, it's kinda personal. I mean it's about a surprise. I better wait and talk to your husband."

I had completely blown it and we both knew it. I dreaded the moment Sloan got wind of this.

He would surely enjoy proving my incompetence to the other employees. He would also love to fire me in front of his staff, proving how important it is not to disobey his orders. However, I could not let that happen today.

Mrs. Nolan said OK and we hung up. I was standing out by the front showcase when the phone rang. Before I could grab it and say hello, Jennifer was answering, "Good morning, Caribbean Jewelry Co."I saw her blank look as she placed the phone back on the receiver.

She caught me looking, shrugged her shoulders and said, "They hung up on me."

I knew immediately who it had been. Mrs. Nolan now knew

someone from the jewelry store was calling her husband.

I spent most of that day watching Sloan and Gray. They were cool, calm and professional. The only problem was, they were professional murderers and I knew it. All I could think about was putting Sloan and Gray away for life. The money from the widow really didn't matter anymore. Well, maybe it did a little. Limbo and I had to get proof.

While waiting for a phone call from Mr. Nolan, I came up with a plan. It involved Limbo and his wife. I needed to find him a wife real fast. Limbo was low key enough not to be recognized. Besides, he had never been in Caribbean Jewelers before. His spouse would be more difficult to locate. Not only did she have to be non-recognizable, she had to be willing to go along with our scheme. It was a dangerous part with little reward. I was hoping Limbo would have a lady in mind. As I thought about it, I wondered if Limbo had any special women in his life. He always seemed to have the ladies dropping by his house and calling him up. However, he had never mentioned any permanent relationship in his life. I'd ask about it later.

Captain Limbo needed to buy his bitch of a wife, whoever she might be, *The Reef* from Mr. Sloan. I had already learned enough about the routine to help coach the unhappy couple. Between now and the time Limbo came in, I would figure a way to video the sale without their knowledge.

I decided to give Limbo a call.

"Hey, Limbo, what are you doing at home in the middle of the day?" I asked.

"Well, I'm going over my notes, trying to sort out all this stuff we've dug up so far. Besides, if you didn't think I was here, why did ya call?" He had a point.

"I've got a plan we need to go over. I could use some help figuring it out," I said.

He told me he was going to be in Key West that evening and suggested meeting him at Captain Tony's Saloon when I got off work. He assured me that in the early evening the bar would not be crowded and we could sit in the back, unnoticed.

"Sounds good. I'll see ya there about six thirty," I said.

A little before five, I was called to the back office.

"A Mr. Howard Nolan is on line one and is not happy," said Jenny.

"Thanks, Jenny, and by the way, you are looking quite fine today," I told her.

"Forget it, Powell, and answer the phone," replied the iron maiden, as she handed me the telephone.

"Hello, Mr. Nolan, this is Powell Taylor." That's as far as I was able to get when he interrupted in a very upset tone.

"My wife said your jewelry store called and wouldn't tell her what it was all about."

I tried to apologize as I explained what had happened. I began with how Mr. Sloan was going to bill him for the tennis bracelet if he did not come pay off his account in full. I then tried to explain how I was stuck with no explanation earlier on the phone with Mrs. Nolan. I told him I was quite sure his wife called the telephone number I had given her and hung up when she realized whom it was.

He was becoming more and more angry. I told him I was upset all day thinking about it and that I had come up with the perfect solution. He was all ears.

"Tell your wife that you won a free pair of diamond earrings and it was going to be a surprise for her. Act upset with us, which shouldn't be too difficult, for ruining her surprise. Next, come on in and buy a pair of diamond earrings, pay off your account and take your wife out to dinner where you can give her the earrings. We take all credit cards and I'll give you a special price on the diamonds. Your wife will be happy, you'll be out of a delicate situation and Mr. Sloan will be thrilled you paid your account."

He finally agreed it was the best solution. He said he would see me before closing.

Mr. Nolan must have flown down U.S. 1, from Big Pine Key. He entered the store exactly eighteen minutes after we had hung up the phone. I knew because I was watching the clock in anticipation. I was just as eager to settle this problem as Mr. Nolan was. The whole time I was helping Howard Nolan, Sloan was glaring at me. The look said, "I'll rid that meddling asshole of his job once and for all."

I quickly wrote the receipts and got Mr. Nolan out of the store as soon as I could. The door had hardly closed, before I explained what had happened to Mr. Sloan.

"Mr. Nolan came in and paid off his account early. While he was here, I sold him a pair of nice half carat diamond earrings," I said with a smile.

"How did he pay for the earrings?" asked Mr. Happy

"He paid cash for everything Mr. Sloan. He's really a nice guy," I said, knowing it would aggravate the shit out of him.

Sloan snarled, turned and walked out.

"What a first class asshole," I thought.

Arriving before Limbo, I sat on a designated stool at the bar in Captain Tony's Saloon off Duval Street. The worn brass plate with barely visible block letters read "MEL FISHER." The place was nearly empty. Hazy smoke hung two feet below the humming motor of the ceiling fan. As I waited for Limbo I began to think about Mel Fisher and the life he led. I met him once, a month earlier. I was sitting one stool to starboard. Mel was crouched over the bar where my Corona now sits. The man was already a legend. I had read about him, seen him on Johnny Carson and watched his *National Geographic* special on television. A modern day pirate, he spent his entire life searching for that treasure chest. With fame and fortune, also came disaster and sorrow. He found the sunken galleon, but he lost a son who drowned at the site. When face-to-face with Mel Fisher, you can sense his triumph and also the sadness there in his eyes. I wondered if he sat and thought about his life and tried to make sense of it all. Then I realized maybe that's why he had his own bar stool in Capt'n Tony's Saloon.

Limbo showed up on my third Corona. We moved to a booth in the back. It was just light enough to see an occasional mouse slide across the dingy tile floor.

"So what's this great plan you've come up with?" Limbo asked.

I described to Limbo everything I could remember about Harry and Agnes's behavior while purchasing *The Reef*. We discussed, analyzed and hashed out every angle possible for Limbo's story. When we had finished, we had two major problems. First, we didn't have a wife for Limbo to kill off. Second, we needed seven hundred fifty thousand dollars cash to pay Sloan for *The Reef*.

Yeah, we had a great plan. We were a hundred and fifty thousand short, and we needed a woman willing to risk her life.

Limbo said he was fairly sure he could get another couple of hundred thousand dollars out of the widow. After discussing it, I was sure Limbo was correct—the widow would do anything to divert suspicion from herself. Limbo would go by and tell her our entire plan. She would not have a clue that we knew she was involved in her husband's death. And, if she thought it would help put Sloan away, she would give up more of her inheritance. We were confident that our only obstacle now was to find Limbo a wife.

"Hey, Limbo, let's face that problem mañana," I said.

"Yeah, Powell, mañana!" Limbo answered.

"By the way, Powell," Limbo continued. "Do you know what the translation of mañana is?"

"It means tomorrow," I said.

"Nope, not here in the Keys," Limbo said smiling. "Here in the Keys mañana means maybe tomorrow, maybe not, but definitely not right now! Nobody's in a hurry in da Keys."

"OK, Limbo," I said. "Let's find you a wife tomorrow!"

He nodded.

Boy, was I delightfully surprised when I reached Cudjoe Key and saw the license tag on the Mazda in my front yard. I jumped from my car and rushed to the front door, then I looked back and saw my car rolling down the street. In my haste to see Dawn, I failed to put the gear in park. I turned quickly and began chasing my truck down the hill. Barely missing Mrs. Whipple's new red Cadillac, it jumped the curb, smashed her trash cans and came to a sudden stop when the back bumper slammed into a giant coconut palm.

Feeling embarrassed and hoping no one had seen what I had just done, I picked up Mrs. Whipple's trash, started up my car and returned home once again.

The door opened and the silhouette of my dreams filled the opening. We embraced each other for hours. We talked. Dawn missed me as much as I did her. We were meant to be together and I would never let her leave me. From the looks of her mountain of luggage and belongings, she agreed. Life could not be more beautiful.

Chapter Twelve——

Limbo's visit with the widow went better than either of us had dreamed. "She was listening to every word like her life depended on it," Limbo told me.

"I confessed to her, told her all we knew about Frank Davidson, Harry and their spouses. I told her how *The Reef* was a facade to collect insurance monies. I told her just enough to get her to come up with the extra cash. It worked, Powell. The icing on the cake was when I told her that we suspected Sloan might even try to put the blame on her. I said he was just sleazy enough to try something so low. She ran to the back room and returned with this shopping bag." Limbo tossed a bulging Fast-Buck Freddie's bag on the table. It took us about ten minutes to count out the additional four hundred thousand dollars.

She had paid us a million dollars total now. Limbo and I both knew that chances were we would not collect the second million. The worst case scenario was we would buy *The Reef* for seven hundred fifty thousand dollars and never see that money again. We would have one hundred twenty-five thousand dollars each and *The Reef*.

We entertained a few other options. One: we keep the entire

million dollars, drop the case and tell the widow we know the truth about her, Sloan and the killings. That just happened to be my favorite plan. I could stick five hundred thousand dollars in the bank and Dawn and I could live a stylish life in the Keys.

Limbo beamed me back to earth quickly.

"We would be no better than they are," he scolded. "Besides, the widow wouldn't let us get away with it. She'd probably tell Sloan that we suspected him and Gray. I'm sure she can be quite convincing when necessary. She could also easily turn the tables on us, then we would be the hunted. For the moment, we have a few things on our side, Powell, including the widow's cash, her greed and her determination to take Sloan out of this picture," Limbo said.

"OK, OK," I said. "But if we're going to buy *The Reef* in an effort to trap Sloan and Gray, we need to figure a way to collect our other million dollars, before they arrest the widow."

"Let's work on it," Limbo said.

The next day, Friday, at two-thirty sharp, Mr. and Mrs. James Adams entered the Caribbean Jewelry Co. Limbo was dressed as if he just stepped off his one hundred-foot yacht. He reminded me of Thurston Howell III of *Gilligan's Island*. The gold buttons on his blue blazer reflected red from Dawn's strapless dress. His white slacks and deck shoes added to his more than convincing performance. When he talked, he even sounded like Mr. Howell. Dawn looked radiant with her slinky dress that stopped a good five inches short of her knees. With no hose, no bra, and no tan lines, she was stunning.

I let Jenny approach them first. I heard her ask, "May I help you?"

"Yes, ma'am," Limbo said. "I'm Dr. James Adams, and this is my wife, Dawn."

Before Limbo could finish, Dawn said, "James, do you have to tell everybody in the world that you're a doctor, I mean, who gives a shit anyway? Why can't you just say you're James Adams? Who in the hell are you trying to impress? Let's face it, you're not a brain surgeon, you teach English."

What a fine performance. Limbo calmed her down and asked to see the owner. Jenny scurried to the back and after a few moments returned with Sloan. I felt sure she had told him about Dawn.

If our plan was going to work, Sloan would have to escort Limbo and Dawn back to his office. Earlier I had implemented phase one of our scheme. Limbo knew exactly what book on the shelf I had hidden the video camera behind. He would pretend to be interested in Sloan's library, then reach behind *Famous Gemstones of the World* and flip on the camera. Later, when I would be called in to revise the appraisal, I could easily retrieve the camera along with the incriminating tape. I caught myself smiling as I thought of how ingenious this plan really was.

"How much?" Mrs. Adams yelled as Sloan pointed to *The Reef.*

"James, you are feeling either guilty, stupid, or both. There is no way in hell I want that glob of gold sitting in my living room, especially for seven hundred and fifty thousand dollars."

"Settle down, dear. Besides, it's an investment. The price is bound to increase over the next couple of years."

Dawn was convincing as she stomped and fussed and walked to the other side of the sales floor.

Limbo then said, "Could we please go somewhere private, Mr. Sloan?"

"Sure, Dr. Adams. Let's go back to my office and discuss payment."

Limbo was quite urbane as the two of them disappeared behind the closed door of Sloan's office. Dawn's eye caught mine as we both smiled. I was nervous, but after what seemed to be hours, Limbo and Sloan returned. I looked at my watch. They had been in a conference for about twenty-two minutes. They all shook hands and Limbo said to Sloan, "I'll see you Monday morning bright and early."

"I'll be looking forward to it," Sloan replied.

Then Sloan, just like clockwork, ordered me to his office to redo the names and address on the appraisal of *The Reef.* I remember thinking how easily everything had fallen into place. I slipped the video camera and tape into my briefcase, ignored the unsigned appraisal forms and left the building.

I did not want to arrive home at the same time as Limbo and

Dawn. Maybe I was getting a case of paranoia, but if someone suspected anything, I shouldn't be seen with the loving couple. I stopped on Big Coppitt Key at the Mini Mart to pick up some Coronas, limes, O'Douls for Limbo, and a family sized box of Orville's microwave popcorn. Then I stopped by Coco's Cantina to say hello to the guys and calm my nerves. Carlos was busy in the kitchen. Flora and I sat at the bar discussing a little of everything while sipping some extra strong con leche.

I called Limbo from the restaurant. He said, "Dawn and I'll meet you at your house in ten minutes. We'll park at the marina and walk over."

"Good idea, Limbo, I don't think any of us should be seen together until this is over," I said, and he agreed.

Like a couple of kids sneaking into a theater, Limbo and Dawn slipped through my back door minutes after I had arrived. I popped the popcorn, complete with plenty of salt and butter, poured the brews into some frosted mugs and slipped the tape into the VCR.

"Show time," I announced, and what a performance it was—Academy Award material.

When the camera clicked on, Limbo's face was inches from the lens. He was muttering some small talk about Sloan's fine library. As he turned to face Sloan, Limbo said, "Well, Mr. Sloan, let's get down to why I'm here."

"Be careful now, Mr. Adams. I'm only selling you a piece of art here."

"Cut the smoke screen, Sloan, we both know why I'm here and what I'm buying with my seven hundred fifty thousand dollars," Limbo said in a forceful tone.

"How did you hear about my jewelry store?" Sloan asked.

"Let me put it this way, Mr. Sloan, I was impressed with the purchases made by Frank Davidson, and Harry and Agnes, ah, um, whoever. What difference does it make anyway? They got a real value and I'm looking for the same deal."

"I understand, Mr. Adams. *The Reef* is indeed a value at seven hundred and fifty thousand dollars. As soon as you pay me, you can start to enjoy its beauty."

"Here's what I want, Mr. Sloan. I'll want to give you two hundred and fifty thousand dollars now and the balance of the money after I'm sure of my enjoyment," Limbo said.

"I stopped the VCR and asked Limbo, "Why didn't you just say you would pay him after your wife was eliminated?"

"Powell, you can see he's playing some kind of mind game. He doesn't want to admit out loud that he is murdering folks. Besides, this way it's not too obvious and we don't want to alarm him or scare him off," Limbo said.

"OK, OK." I continued the tape.

"James, there are two things I worry most about in business. Number one is to satisfy my customer. The second is collecting my fee. Therefore, if I'm paid in advance, I can concentrate one hundred percent on number one."

Limbo walked over to the book case as if he were playing to the camera and said, "OK, Mr. Sloan, I'll pay you the other half-million Monday morning. Here's the down payment."

Limbo handed him the bag and we listened as Sloan counted every dollar.

"Fine, James, we have a deal. By the way, you won an offshore three-day fishing trip to the Tortugas. Here's the boat captain's name and phone number. I'll let you know when it's set up," Sloan said as he handed Limbo a business card. They left the room. Dawn and I gave the performance a standing ovation. Limbo smiled, bowed and said, "First of all, I'd like to thank my mother."

We all had a laugh.

We decided to make more copies of the tape, one for Limbo, one for me, one for the FBI and this one for the widow. We thought we would show and sell the fourth video tape to the lady who hired us. It was a perfect idea. She would jump at the chance to have proof against Sloan. We would collect our outstanding million in exchange for that proof.

"Let's finish this conversation later, Limbo," I said. "I'm tired. By the way, would you mind if your beautiful wife stayed here with me tonight?"

"I guess not, Powell," Limbo said as he was leaving.

After a long passionate shower, Dawn and I sat in bed together for hours talking. We discussed our future together, agreeing on every detail. Right before we dozed off, Dawn said, "I think I'm going to apply for a job at the First Bank of The Keys in Key West."

"Great!" I said. I'll bring my duffle bag of cash and open a new account."

"Powell, you can't just walk in a bank and deposit a hundred and twenty-five thousand dollars."

"Why not?" I said.

"You just can't. It's not legal! If anyone deposits more than ten thousand dollars in cash, they have to fill out a special form for the IRS. They're cracking down on illegal drug money. Can you explain to the IRS why you have one hundred and twenty-five thousand dollars in cash?"

"No, I reckon not," I said. "What can I do, especially if Limbo and I collect the remainder of the money?"

"You have a couple of choices, Powell. You can deposit nine thousand and nine hundred dollars every day for, let's see, sixty-three days, or you can put it all in an account in the Cayman Islands. You'll have to go by boat, because you could never get on and off an airplane hiding six hundred and twenty-five thousand dollars. Besides, it could be dangerous, walking around with that kind of money."

"Yeah, I guess. We'll worry about all that stuff later," I said. "Good night, Dawn, I love you."

"I love you too, Powell."

It was easier to say than I thought, and even better to listen to.

The alarm clock woke us early. I phoned Sloan at home to tell him I was sick and would not be in to work. I agreed to work my normal day off, Monday, instead. After a long hesitation he mumbled, "OK." I could sense his snarl. As we cooked breakfast I explained to Dawn why I called in sick as we cooked breakfast.

"Now I'll be working Monday morning when your husband, Dr. James Adams, picks up *The Reef,* I said.

Limbo came in as we were just finishing. I brewed some more coffee and cooked up another conch and cheese omelet.

"This is some great coffee, Powell, where did you get it," Limbo asked.

"I got it from Carlos. I think it's a Cuban bean he gets out of Miami," I replied. "Bustello, I think."

With the chit chat out of the way we had "bidness" to attend to, as Walter-Mon would say.

We made plans for the weekend. After visiting with our employer, the widow, we would plan Sloan's destiny. Hopefully we would also have another problem to overcome: what to do with six hundred and twenty-five thousand dollars in cash, each. It was a dilemma I welcomed.

That evening about ten o'clock we finally hooked up with the widow. Limbo introduced me as his partner, who was working undercover in Sloan's Jewelry store. She was not impressed and seemed to be in a foul mood. I believe she sensed that we were back to collect more money. Although we explained explicitly every move we were making, it was not until we plugged the tape in her TV that her attitude changed for the better.

"Yes! Yes, guys, that's what I wanted. We got that son of a bitch now." Limbo asked her for the next million dollars.

He said, "Give us the money and we'll never see one another again. You'll be reading about Sloan and Gray in the papers real soon. If it doesn't work out and we fail, there will be no ties between us. Of course, if it doesn't work out, you'll probably be reading our obituary in the paper."

"How do I know you won't just take the money and run?" she asked.

"Cause I'm giving you this tape to keep for your very own. As you can see, I'm one of the main stars in it. I certainly don't want you to hand it over to the authorities," Limbo said in a convincing tone.

"Can I trust you gentleman? Lets face it, how do I know you'll carry out the plan?" she continued.

Limbo used Sloan's philosophy.

"Well, ma'am, the two main things on my mind are making you happy and collecting that money. If I get paid fully in advance, Powell and I can concentrate a hundred percent on the business at hand," he said.

She went to the back room for a few moments. Limbo took the tape out of the VCR, swapped it for a blank one and left it on the coffee table. When she returned this time, Limbo didn't count the contents of the sack of money the widow brought with her. He grabbed it. As we were leaving, Limbo told our ex-employer, "It was nice doing business with you. When you look at that tape again, you're probably not going to like what you see. But, it's the price you pay for not telling us the whole story. If we ever hear a word out of you we'll show this to the FBI," Limbo said as he held up the photo from Deep Water Cay. "You didn't tell us you were with Sloan and Gray when your husband disappeared. Frankly, I don't think prop cuts look anything at all like shark bites. You'll never hear from us again, ma'am."

"You mother fuckers, you." She said it with a slight smile on her face.

I was still shaking on our trip back home. I didn't like the fact that the widow knew who we were and how we had conned her out of twenty percent of her inheritance. By the time we reached Cudjoe, Limbo had almost convinced me we had nothing to fear.

"She would be a fool to try and cross us now, Powell," Limbo said. "She knows we've got her by the short hairs. She'll make no waves, I promise." For a reason I could not explain I felt dishonest, even dirty. I was thinking that the proper thing to do would be to turn the money over to the authorities and tell them the whole story. The widow is just as guilty as Sloan and Gray.

"Don't you feel like a crook?" I asked as I pointed to the bag of cash. "I mean we got a total of two million dollars from a woman who helped kill her husband. Now she's turning in her accomplices," I continued.

"Look, Powell, it'll all work out. We're doing society a big favor by ridding it of two evil killers," Limbo said unconvincingly.

"But we're leaving one murderer on the streets," I added.

"Powell, ours is not a perfect world. We have to do the best we can."

"Let's get a good night sleep and talk about it tomorrow."

The next morning, nothing had changed. There was no mystical awakening that transformed the way I felt. I was a greedy lowlife, not much better than the murderess who had hired Limbo and me.

The sun was not up yet when I heard a knock at the front door. Limbo and Dawn entered in their Mr. and Mrs. outfits.

Limbo said, "Powell, we need to talk before you head to work."

"After looking into the widow's case I learned a great deal about her husband and Sloan that I didn't tell you. They were the lowest of lows. Not only did her husband beat her unmercifully, he forced her to have sex with Sloan and others while he video taped the performance. He often got drunk and brought home prostitutes, forcing his wife to join them in group sex. When she complained, he beat her. She has been hospitalized more than fifteen times; twice she almost died of internal bleeding. That's not the worst of it either. One of his latest whores gave the couple a little going away gift. The main reason the widow was so eager to give us the two million dollars is because she hasn't got enough time left to spend the money she has. She contracted the HIV virus from one of the many scumbags forced on her."

"I thought you once told me Sloan's partner and the widow loved each other and went everywhere together," I said.

"That was before your trip to the Bahamas, Powell. That was before I suspected the widow. I dug up all of this since that trip," Limbo said.

This new evidence was not convincing. I didn't know if I should believe it or not. It seemed a bit too convenient. After another thirty minutes I was somewhat sure Limbo believed his own story, and was sticking to it. I wanted to believe him. I wanted to hate the dead man. It would get me off the hook, set me free and ease my mind.

"By George, I believe you, Limbo. The widow's dead husband was one awful son of a bitch. He deserved everything he got, and I'm keeping every penny of the money. That poor woman, what a shame."

Chapter Thirteen —

I spent the best part of the morning trying to decide the most advantageous way to retire from the Caribbean Jewelry Company. If Limbo and Dawn were going on a long fishing trip set up by Sloan, I needed to be close behind.

Although I feared for Jenny, I thought it best to tell her nothing. The less she knew, the safer she would be. Whereas Jenny and I never really established a relationship, I felt that in a different time and different place we might have been close.

As I was trying to think up reasons to quit, I watched a grandiose metamorphosis at the front door. Limbo and Dawn walked in as Doctor and Mrs. James Adams, alias Thurston Howell III and his lovely wife.

Jenny looked my way and rolled her eyes as if to say, "Not this bitch again," as she directed the couple to Sloan's office. It was only a few seconds before the couple returned to the front door. Limbo had traded his briefcase for a beautiful gold sculpture. As they left, the Mrs. was a-griping and a-bitching. Another flagrant but fine performance.

Mr. Sloan then gave me the perfect opportunity to exit without casting a shadow of suspicion.

"Powell, could you step back here for a moment?" he said.

"I need you to sign this appraisal for Doctor and Mrs. Adams," he continued.

Reading over the description I realized it was my very own appraisal of *The Reef*, from my job interview. The bottom line replacement value was seven hundred seventy-five thousand dollars. This was my chance, I thought.

"Sorry, Mr. Sloan, but I can't sign this appraisal. It's not accurate. The replacement value is way too inflated. You know as well as I do it's only worth one-ninety to two hundred thousand, tops." Although he was turning beet red and his snarl twitched nervously, I continued. "I don't know how you get away with it, Sloan. You are not an ethical person," I said as he exploded.

"Get your pompous, mother-fucking, ass out of my store and don't ever step foot in here again," he yelled as he pushed me out into a showcase. I hit the showcase, fell to the floor, swung back around, and clipped Sloan behind both knees forcing him to the carpet. I jumped up, put my foot to his throat and said, "You'll get yours one day. I only hope I'm there to see it, you asshole."

At that moment Harrison Gray grabbed my neck, spun me around and knocked me out the front door with one punch between my eyes. Through bloodied eyes I saw Jenny run out the door. I motioned her back inside and told her I would call her tonight.

So much for my inconspicuous departure. When I stopped at Coco's Cantina on the way home, Denise brought me a cold Corona and a bag of ice. I sipped the beer and held the ice to my forehead. My eyes had already begun to swell. After finishing the beer I went straight home. I had a few phone calls to make. My first call was to Gulf Breeze, Florida.

"Charles, Sr., please," I said.

A "Hello?" answered on the other end.

"Dad, hey it's me, Powell. How ya doing?"

"Good Powell, what's wrong?" Sr. said.

"What cha mean, Dad?"

"I know something is wrong Powell. It's four o'clock in the afternoon, I haven't heard a peep out of you in five weeks and I know you're not just calling to say hi."

He always was pretty knowledgeable at reading people. That was one of his strong points in business. He could tell who was honest, who would make a good employee and who would pay their bills. I always believed that to be his biggest asset in business. He could definitely read people.

"Well, Dad, you're right. I had a rough day today. Sloan just fired me for not signing an inflated appraisal. Do you remember that gold sculpture I told you about?"

"Yeah, Powell, the one you said was worth one hundred and ninety thousand dollars and Sloan placed its value at seven hundred and fifty?"

"That's the one," I replied.

"Well, son, don't worry about it. You did the right thing. I'm proud of you. Fuck Sloan."

I couldn't believe my ears. Not only was it the first time I'd ever heard him say fuck, but it was also the first time he ever said he was proud of me.

"Thanks, Dad."

"You OK, son?" he asked.

"Yeah, I'm OK Dad. I'll give you a call Thursday night at home."

"OK, I'll talk to you then, Powell. Goodbye."

"Goodbye," I said as I hung up, still wondering why I couldn't bring myself to tell him how I felt.

I laid on the bed for a moment to collect my thoughts and meditate. I was about to doze off when I heard the back door slam. I jumped up and peered through the small crack in the door. I was relieved to see Limbo and Dawn. When I opened my door, Dawn ran over, kissed me and gave me a strong hug using her whole body.

"Why you home so early?" Limbo asked.

After I carefully explained the whole incident to them, Limbo said, "Good, Powell, that'll work out just right. I was wondering how you were going to get off Thursday."

"What's happening Thursday, Limbo?"

He told me that Thursday was the day he and Dawn were to go charter fishing out of Key West. Sloan had set up a three-day trip for Dr. and Mrs. James Adams, to fish the waters off the Dry

Tortugas. I read aloud from the business card Limbo handed me—
"Charter Fishing aboard the *Gold Digger*."

Limbo told me he had also chartered another boat for me.

My twenty-seven-foot center-console with twin 225s was docked at Murray's Marina, also the home of the thirty-eight-foot *Gold Digger*.

For the remainder of the evening the three of us merely sat around not saying much. I never had the chance to call Jenny and explain my sudden exit earlier. I believe it was our anticipation of the day to come that had us all in a sullen, nervous timbre. With the welcome silence, came much thought. Flashing through my mind were plenty of what ifs. What if Gray and Sloan succeeded in the disappearance of Mr. and Mrs. Adams? If Sloan suspected our involvement, Limbo and I could be a link in the ocean's food chain by the weekend. Charles, Sr., Imogene and Brad would never be able to understand the truth. Why did I let Dawn get involved? Did I really believe Limbo's story about the mistreated widow?

What had happened to my dreams of guiding and traveling throughout the Keys?

Besides helping me delve deep into my inner soul and reminisce as my life flashed before me, the quietness of the evening told me something else. The ceiling fan overhead needed some oil. Like the chirp of a cricket, the squeaky motor was an obvious distraction. I caught myself staring at the second hand on my watch. In one minute I counted thirty-four annoying squeals.

I snapped out of my trance when Limbo said, "Powell, you and Dawn need to meet me at the Navy base on Boca Chica Key at ten-thirty tomorrow morning. I've set up an appointment with Customs to explain everything and ask for some help for the weekend."

"Do you think it's wise for Dawn to stay here with me tonight?" I asked. I was happy with his reply. Limbo said he was sure no one suspected anything and that we were about to put an end to all of our worries. Customs would see to that.

"Get some sleep and I'll see you at ten-thirty tomorrow," Limbo said.

I knew it was risky for Dawn and me to be seen together, but I sure was happy she stuck around that night.

The next morning while Dawn was in the shower, I was in the

kitchen pouring a cup of coffee. There was a little tap at the front door. I wish now that I had ignored it.

When I opened the door, Jenny jumped across the threshold and latched onto me as if never to let go. As I was easing her away from me Jenny said, "Powell, I'm so sorry about yesterday. Mr. Sloan had no right to treat you like that. And for what it's worth, I think you were right not to sign that appraisal." I smiled and was about to thank her when the bathroom door flew open. Jenny and I both turned. Dawn was standing there with a quickly disappearing smile in nothing but her panties, naked from the waist up. She and Jenny screamed at the same time. Dawn returned to the bathroom slamming the door behind her.

"Who the hell was that, Powell?" Jenny barked. "She looks, familiar, do I know her, Powell?"

Before I could answer, she had disappeared. A few seconds later I heard her car tires burning rubber as she pulled out onto U. S. 1.

It took the entire twenty-minute ride to the Navy Base to explain to Dawn who the girl was who caught an entire upper body shot of her. I only hoped Jenny would not link the gorgeous, bare-breasted, wet-haired Dawn with the vivacious blonde lady named Mrs. James Adams.

Captain Limbo waited for us at the main gate of Boca Chica Naval Base. Escorting him, were two very important looking officers in spotless uniforms. After parking our car, all three of us were transported by jeep to a building on the far end of the base.

Our arrival had definitely been anticipated. Inside the building we sat at a mammoth conference table near a wall of huge windows. Gazing outside, I could see the Atlantic less than ten feet away.

Limbo sat at the center of the table flanked by the two uniforms on either side. Dawn and I were across from them. I counted about thirty empty chairs surrounding us in the almost vacant building. We were alone, private, all would be confidential. For some insane reason, I felt safer. It must have been just knowing that we had the authorities on our side that helped. We were legitimate. Limbo and I were doing the honest and honorable thing here. I was feeling good.

As Limbo stood to begin, a splash on the flats caught my eye.

It was a black tail, slicing through the shallows in a search of an appetizing snack. From my seat, it appeared to be a small blacktip shark, lashing around for food. "Let's get started," Limbo said.

For an hour and a half Limbo laid out our past, lengthy investigation to the two officials. The officer to Limbo's left was Customs. The gent to his right was proudly Coast Guard.

For the most part, Dawn and I were silent. Ever so often, Limbo would ask me a question or for my opinion on a particular matter. Limbo was surprisingly prepared. By the time he'd finished we had outlined an accurate picture of Sloan, Gray and their money-making murders. We had somehow left out the widow and the amount of the reward.

The Coast Guard and Customs were happy to offer their assistance.

Captain Coast Guard said, "We'll place some unmarked boats in the waters between Key West and the Tortugas. We'll monitor channel 65 on the radio."

I said I would leave my radio tuned to 65 and would keep a close watch on the *Gold Digger* and its crew. Limbo said he would try to make sure the crew did not listen to channel 65. The agent from Customs said he would place two officers at Fort Jefferson in the Dry Tortugas. He also said Customs would have two sea planes on standby.

When we were leaving the building, I noticed two additional fins searching for nourishment near the shore. I motioned to Limbo as I pointed to the fish.

"Look at those sharks," I said.

"Powell, look again," Limbo replied. "Those aren't sharks."

For the past two hours I'd been watching permit cruising the flats for crabs. That was the one fish I had yet to catch on a fly. Although I'd had many shots, I still had never landed one, and had the utmost respect for these large, silver relatives of the jack family.

After a little pleading, I convinced Limbo to arrange for my return later that afternoon. He knew how badly I wanted to catch a permit. Although he didn't say so, Limbo probably was thinking this might be my last chance to realize that dream. Thursday could change our lives drastically or, worse yet, end them forever.

Limbo, Dawn, and I agreed we should not be seen together until after this was all over. I kissed Dawn, wished her good luck on Thursday and told her how much I loved her.

She told me to be careful and how happy she would be when our lives could become normal again. Her eyes were teary.

My eyes also began to fill when she drove off with Limbo. If anything happened to her, I could never forgive myself. To stave off second thoughts, I rushed home, got my ten-weight rod, my fly reel and a couple of great looking crab patterns I had tied up. My favorite one was a pattern I had devised myself, after many hours of trial and error. It was a combination of many crab patterns with a few new ideas of my own. I named it after Charles, Sr. I called it "Crabmudgeon."

After a quick twenty-minute ride, my Dodge pickup, with its smashed rear bumper from Mrs. Whipple's palm tree, delivered me to the entrance of the Navy base. The sailor at the front gate saluted me through. I parked my truck at the building, where I had spent most of the day and walked out to the shore. The permit were still there, frolicking and feeding in about a foot of water as if they were a thousand miles from civilization. I stopped about seventy feet away; any closer and I was sure to spook them. With just one back cast, I dropped the crabmudgeon directly between the noses of two nice fish.

I saw the one on the left shoot across the flat at the speed of sound, throwing spray all the way. I had him hooked and he was headed for deeper water.

I kept constant pressure on him, trying to retrieve some of the two hundred feet of line he had stripped off on his first run. He was a magnificent fish, about thirty to thirty-five pounds.

Just when I was feeling confident about landing my first permit on fly, a large dorsal fin appeared on the flat fifty feet away. Although I couldn't see the shark's body, I could imagine his bluntly rounded snout slashing from side to side beneath the surface in search of my panicked and helpless permit. I couldn't risk such a magnificent fish. I clamped down on my reel's spool. Sensing danger, the big permit made one more effort to escape. Because I held tight to the reel, the fish broke the ten-pound tippet. He was free. His tail disappeared below the surface as he scooted for deeper water as the bull shark thrashed around still looking for supper. Tonight he would not be dining on my permit. I did not feel down about losing that fish. We had both won.

I spent all day Wednesday preparing. In an effort not to cause any suspicions at the dock, I behaved as if I were going on a three-day fishing trip.

Thanks to Charles, Sr., I was quite familiar with what had to be done to prepare for a bottom-fishing expedition. The check list included bait, tackle, ice chest, ice, chum, drinks, food, rods, reels, cameras, sunglasses, sunscreen, chum bag, life jackets, maps and loran book. On this trip I also carried an item I never needed in Gulf Breeze: I packed a thirty-eight Smith and Wesson. I didn't need the pistol for modern-day pirates, or the disgruntled Cubans that sometimes inhabit these waters; I needed it for protection from Captain Harrison Gray aboard Sloan's *Gold Digger*. Although it was only a guess, I was pretty sure Sloan must own the thirty-eight footer.

After loading my truck with the necessities, I decided to call Jenny.

"Caribbean Jewelry Company," an unfamiliar voice answered.

"Can I speak with Jenny, please?"

"I'm sorry, sir. She's not in today." I thanked him and hung up.

When I called Jenny at home, she hung up on me. When I tried to call her back, all I got was a busy signal. She'd taken the phone off the hook. I called her on and off for an hour or so. I finally said the hell with her. I'd tried to get along with her since the day we had met. Now, she didn't want anything to do with me. Although she said she wasn't involved with anyone, she acted otherwise. The hell with it, I wouldn't lose sleep over her. Besides, I was more worried about Dawn and her role in our risky venture.

What would I like for my last supper? Coco's, of course. I paid a late-night visit to see Carlos, Flora and Denise. I think that night, Carlos sensed my nervousness. Which probably explains why he insisted on joining me for supper. He and Flora sat with me as Denise took our orders and Phillipe relieved Carlos in the kitchen.

"Try the special tonight, Powell. I'm sure you'll like it," Flora said.

We all had the special: fried pork chunks, black beans and rice,

Cuban bread and fried plantains. I ate so much I had no room for flan or even a cup of con leche. Besides, I didn't want any caffeine to keep me awake all night. Carlos did not let me pay for my meal. I thanked him and told Flora that she and Carlos were my "Keys family" and that I appreciated everything they'd done for me.

As I dozed off that night, I hoped I'd see my friends and family again. I felt the dark touch of fear. All my life, the black of night stripped away the protection daylight seemed to provide. And this night brought with it not only fear, but my prayers, prayers almost forgotten over the past few years.

Chapter Fourteen —

I woke up about four-thirty, a good hour and a half before the sun peeked over the horizon. Although I'd gotten a great night of sleep, I needed no alarm clock to wake me. My eyes popped open and I was already deep in thought about the risky day ahead. My subconscious had taken over, prepared me for my sudden awakening.

When I arrived at Murray's Marina on Stock Island, it was quiet. Taking no chances on being seen or recognized, I quickly loaded my gear, tackle and rations on the boat, filled the ice chest with food, drinks and ice, checked the fuel and made sure I had extra gas and oil. Everything seemed in order.

As I waited for Doctor and Mrs. James Adams to arrive and meet up with Captain Gray, I read the booklet on my rented boat, a Conch 27 with twin 225-horse outboards. According to the specs, she could do sixty-five miles per hour in three-foot seas. I was prepared for battle, if it came to that.

After the sun was up, I could tell it was going to be one of those days fishermen dream of. A mirrored reflection of the early sunlight gleamed across the flat, aqua surface, blinding me for a moment. I put on my long billed hat and sunglasses, started both engines and waited while they warmed up. I was a good ten boat slips away from the *Gold Digger*, and although the large, bold letters on her stern were easily readable I could not make out who was aboard. But I'd remembered to bring my backpack with my birding gear. If I stayed alive long enough to reach the Tortugas, I hoped to spot some of its rare, pelagic birds, I had never seen a brown booby or a masked booby or any of the migrant terns that nest in the Dry Tortugas. That's why I'd brought my binoculars.

In a few minutes with the help of the Bausch and Lombs I could see Limbo and Dawn boarding the *Gold Digger*. Gray was helping them aboard while an unidentified mate handled their gear. I couldn't make out the faces, but I was certain the bodies belonged to Harrison Gray, Limbo and Dawn.

I scanned the marina hoping to see some sign of back up from Captain Coast Guard and his Customs buddies, but saw no familiar faces, until I glanced at the other boats. There was Sloan, idling out of the marina toward open water.

I followed him, hoping that Gray would be leaving soon. Staying three boats behind the stern of Sloan's go-fast boat, I wasn't sure of the boat's brand name, but it was similar to the racing hulls drug dealers use in Miami Vice. We always called them "go- fast boats," most likely a *Scarab*. The exhaust from his huge inboards made a hell of a racket as we idled through the no-wake zone. I did not want to get into a pissing contest with Sloan and his fancy machine.

Looking back beyond my wake, I was happy to see the *Gold Digger* slowly moving out of the harbor. Now I was directly midway between Sloan and Gray. Not a good place to be. Luckily the three of us were idling at about the same speed. I began to think I had the upper hand. I knew who was here and where they were. But, to the best of my knowledge, they did not yet know about me. With my long billed cap and dark fishing glasses I looked like a hundred other anglers.

With one eye forward and the other one aft, I reached up and turned on the boat's electronics. The loran lit up and defined my exact location. The fish-finder and bottom sounder both kicked on.

But when I turned on the radio, nothing happened. It was dead. I wiggled the knobs, played with the squelch button and shook the wires on the back. Nothing, nada, as Carlos would say. My advantage had slipped away, the odds were closer to even.

I heard Sloan's pretty boy boat rev her wicked engines and take off. By the time I reached the end of the no wake zone, Sloan had almost disappeared, on a heading due south. I decided to wait on the *Gold Digger* and forget Sloan, he'd be back.

Twenty minutes after the *Gold Digger* passed me on the starboard side, I reached the sea buoy. Trailing a mile or so behind, I watched through the binoculars as Gray adjusted his course west, toward the Tortugas. My main concern was Sloan. I did not like being out here without a radio and without knowing Sloan's whereabouts. He was a dangerous part of this puzzle that not only did not fit but now was missing totally from the game. That worried me, I feared most for Limbo and Dawn.

Fear for my own life did not come until later. We cruised at about twenty-five knots for an hour after passing the sea buoy. Gray had not altered his course or speed, so I decided to check the radio, one more time. If it worked, I could notify Customs and the Coast Guard, give them our location and speed. Then they'd know when to expect us in the Dry Tortugas.

I unscrewed the front plate on the built in VHF and slid the radio from its bracket. Looking closely, I found a good reason to worry. I had been dreadfully wrong. Someone did know I was here. Somehow they knew what boat I would be on. How else could I explain why all the wires in the radio had been cut in half and the inside smashed. "No, I'm just being paranoid," I told myself. No one could have known.

When he reached the Gulf Stream, Gray slowed his engines and began to fish. As I watched through the glasses I could only figure their reason for trolling was to convince Mrs. Adams they were indeed on a fishing trip.

The water was the richest cobalt blue I'd ever seen. I loved being there, I only wish I could have enjoyed it. This river in the ocean reminded me of a conversation I had one night up at Coco's Cantina. After Frankie Russell finished up her last set and most of the band had gone home, I bought her a few beers and just listened.

One particular story stuck in my mind as I now gazed into the azure waters far south of the Marquesas. Her husband, Joe Russell and Ernest Hemingway were two cronies who often cruised to Cuba from their homes in Key West.

That was during prohibition in the United States, a time when Americans were thirsty. Frankie said the two often carried liquor from Cuba to the Keys.

When my life returned to normal, I would make a special effort to find Frankie and continue our conversation. She had images in the back of her head that I dreamed of discovering and transferring to paper. She probably knew more about the Nobel Prize-writing author than anyone alive. They both interested me.

Just as most people could not understand my fascination with living in the Keys, Hemingway often found himself explaining his own reasons for loving Cuba. Those very reasons were responsible for his decision to leave his home in Key West so he could live in Cuba for twenty-two of his years. Where he enjoyed raising, training and fighting his chickens. Where cockfighting was legal. He liked the wildlife. He loved eating the eighteen different varieties of mangoes that grew on the slope near his home. Like me when I was in the Keys, Hemingway put on shoes only when he went to town.

I'm sure there were many other reasons for his love of Cuba that had somehow slipped my mind. The one I did remember, however, was the reason I liked best.

Hemingway would tell his friends that the reason he lived in Cuba was the great, deep blue river that was only thirty minutes from his door. A mile deep and nearly eighty broad, when the Gulf Stream was right it was the finest fishing the author ever knew.

The *Gold Digger* had adjusted her trolling speed, moving slightly faster now. As I watched the activity, I felt sure that Gray would not try anything until the return trip. For now, Limbo and Dawn were having a great time. They looked like a happily married couple of tourists on the adventure of a lifetime. The mate, whom I realized was a female, was good with the gaff. Dawn and Limbo boated three or four nice wahoo and dolphin in a short time. They seemed to be enjoying themselves. Good actors, I hoped they survived the last act.

I eased the throttle slightly forward in an effort to keep up with Gray. For some reason, I'd been slipping farther and farther behind. Looking around the cockpit of the boat I had an unexplainable feeling that something was wrong. Knowing that someone had sabotaged my radio was probably good cause for my paranoia. While Limbo and Dawn were happy catching fish I decided to take a close look around on my rented boat. Pointing my bow directly at the stern of the *Gold Digger*, I went forward to check the anchor and rope locker. All OK—full of rope and anchor. With the exception of the VHF radio, the electronics were in perfect running condition. One at a time, I took both cowlings off the oversized outboards and checked them closely. For what, I wasn't sure. Nothing seemed out place and I was convinced they were in great shape. There was no visible corrosion or rust. Both engines were well maintained and the spark plugs looked brand new. It is unusual for outboard motors that are run in saltwater not to have any signs of corrosion. Glancing forward toward the *Gold Digger*, I replaced the large detachable covering on the 225-horse Yamaha, squelching the loud engine noise. When I jumped down off the gunwale, I landed on a deck under about three inches of water. That much water was not good, not good at all. Now I knew why the boat had slowed. The hull was full of water, rising past the floor boards. I ran to the console, splashing water with every step. I searched for a switch that ran the bilge pump. Hopefully the automatic switch on the pump was frozen in the "off" position, and it wouldn't allow the pump to come on. I couldn't find any switch to activate the bilge pump. I wondered what this meant. Was I sinking? Did someone put a hole in my hull knowing I would go down before reaching my destination? The water was now ankle deep throughout the whole boat.

Something else was wrong. I saw and heard Sloan's *Scarab* running parallel to the *Gold Digger* a mile ahead. My fears were confirmed. He knew I was here.

I changed course and hit the throttle forward bringing the Conch 27 up on a plane, forcing all the water to the stern, clearing the forward hatch. I unscrewed the hatch cover and there it was: the bilge pump had been rigged with some type of bomb. What looked like sticks of dynamite had been wired to the automatic float device on the pump. Had I found the pump switch, I would have been fish bait. It was a miracle that I was still alive. The plan to blow me up was ingenious. Someone, probably Sloan or Gray, drilled a hole in the bottom of the boat directly beneath the bilge pump. They had wired the bomb to go off when the automatic lever turned the bilge pump on. The water would fill, forcing the lever up, turning on the bilge and BOOM! No more Powell Taylor, no more investigations, and no more looking over their shoulders.

I looked closer just to see what it was that saved my lucky ass. A small clump of monofilament line had jammed the automatic lever, not allowing it to lift when the water entered the hole Sloan had drilled.

I knew that there was no way for me to disarm the bomb or remove the fishing line without blowing me up to where the frigate birds fly.

From reading the boat manual earlier, I knew there was supposed to be a life raft beneath the center console. I was surprised, but happy to see it exactly where it was meant to be.

I guess Sloan didn't figure on me ever realizing what was supposed to happen. He didn't see a need to remove the raft. I should have been blown to hell and back before I knew what was going on. I shut down the outboards and welcomed the silence as I removed the raft from its locker and pulled the cord. Shaking and quivering like a wet dog, it filled with air immediately. Holding the rope that was attached to its bow, I tossed it over the side. Standing atop the starboard gunwale, I paused for a moment before jumping in. Just as I leaped, a random wave hit the bow of the twenty-seven footer jarring loose the mono fishing line and activating the bomb. The last thing I remember as I landed head first in the life raft, was the enormous explosion and the heat of the fire as it burned my skin. Somehow my raft escaped the wrath of the explosion.

Chapter Fifteen ——

As my memory returned, so did my other senses. With a clear mind I now felt hungry and tired. What day was today? How long had I been afloat?

I realized there was only one explanation for the attempt on my life, at least, only one that made sense to me. Jenny recognized Dawn at my house that day. She probably reported back to Sloan. Winston Sloan, not being a dumb man, surely put two and two together, calculated his risks and decided it best to eliminate me. Had I spent twenty seconds longer aboard that boat, he would have succeeded.

As I kept rolling from side to side in an attempt to get comfortable, I wondered just what Jenny knew. How was she involved? Was she just an innocent naive bystander as I hoped or was she helping Sloan somehow?

Then I realized, "Who cares? What difference would it make when they found my decaying carcass stuck to the side of this fucking raft?"

My overwhelming sadness disappeared as quickly as it had

surfaced. I spotted a boat on the horizon. As the boat came closer I knew its crew would not notice me unless I did something to get their attention. Although the boat would pass less than a mile from me, I was a speck floating between waves. There were no flares or paddles aboard. I had no way of flagging them down. But I could not just do nothing. I jumped overboard, grabbed the raft and held it as high in the air as possible while balancing the rounded gunwale on the water. I hoped that the bright yellow sides would get someone's attention. I threw it up and down until my arms gave out. I righted the boat, emptied the water and crawled back aboard. Balancing on my knees, I waved my arms as if I were doing jumping jacks from the waist up. I noticed the bow of the boat change course and head directly toward me. I sat down, grinned a big one and waited.

I thought, "How apropros" when the Sportfisher got close enough for me to read the name *Look Out* on her bow. I was thankful that she lived up to her name.

"Hey! I'm Captain Gainey Maxwell. You OK down there?" A crusty voice yelled out.

"Yes, sir and boy am I glad to see you," I answered.

He threw me a rope ladder which I scaled in seconds.

"Captain Gainey, my name is Powell Taylor and I'm very pleased to make your acquaintance," I said as I shook his hand frantically. My mind was spinning. I was half way listening to the captain as he introduced Dr. and Mrs. So and So with their two boys. I did manage to hear him say they lived in New Jersey. I smiled, wondering if Captain Gainey shared the same sentiments about New Jerseyians as Captain Ed Walker did. The two boys were identical twins about twelve or thirteen years old. They sat together, very attentive.

With their starched shirts and matching pants, Nike tennis shoes and white socks to their knees, they looked as if they were awaiting Sister Mary Consuela to teach them religion. I felt a little sadness for them.

"We're headed for the Tortugas for a week of fishing," Gainey said. "You can catch a ride back with the Key West Seaplane Service. They have two or three flights a day this time of year. I'm sure one of them will have room for you," he continued.

Captain Gainey told me I could stay aboard the *Look Out* this evening and catch a plane in the morning. The first Cessna on floats would show up about ten a. m.

"That's great and I really appreciate the ride," I said. "By the way," I continued. "What day is it?"

Today was Friday. Although I had only been afloat about eight hours, it felt like weeks. My dark hide hadn't been caused by the sun's rays. That leathery skin peeling from my body was a result of the explosion.

I'm sure Captain Gainey and his crew were more than curious about why I was drifting thirty miles offshore in a rubber dinghy. Their inquisitive minds seemed satisfied with my lame explanation. Earlier, I had told them I was headed to the Tortugas to fish when I hit some floating debris.

"A log pierced my bow, barely giving me time to inflate my raft before she went down," I told them. It was weak, but they bought it just the same.

"Do you need to call anyone and let them know you're OK?" Gainey asked.

I started to say no. Right then my brain began to word again.

"Yes, sir, I sure would. Could I call my girlfriend?" I said.

He pointed to the flying bridge and said I could use the radio up there. I ran up the aluminum rungs and switched the VHF to channel 65.

"This is Powell Taylor, are you there?" I whispered into the mike.

"This is Customs, where the hell are you, why haven't you called before now?"

I gave them a quick recap. I told them about the bomb and explosion. They were happy I found my way aboard the *Look Out*.

I described Sloan's *Scarab* and the *Gold Digger* to them.

"I believe they're both headed to the Tortugas," I said.

It was a good thing I called them. Not hearing from Limbo or myself, they had aborted the mission. They would send a plane out as soon as they could fuel up and get a crew.

I warned them to be cautious. I didn't want Sloan or Gray to become suspicious. For all they knew, I was dead and no one else knew their whereabouts. It was important for Customs not be seen on the island. If Sloan and Gray tried to kill me, they certainly knew Limbo was involved. Captain Customs agreed. Before I switched the VHF back to channel sixteen, I told them I would try and call them about ten o'clock tonight to check in.

When I returned to the deck, the Mrs. was sitting in the fighting chair cranking in a fish on a huge gold colored reel. There was no fight. The reel, probably spooled with eighty-pound line, outranked the small kingfish ten to one. The couple from New Jersey were ecstatic as they hooted and hollered. The poor fish was almost baked enough to eat by the time the camera quit. The two twins with their saffron colored pompadours sat motionlessly without expression. I couldn't stand it any longer. If I was going to sit here patiently and watch this family fish, they were going to have fun. Noticing that Captain Gainey was alone with no help, I yelled up; "Captain, mind if I mate for ya?"

"No, that would be great, Powell," he answered. He said his mate had not shown up for work this morning. Rather than cancel his trip, Gainey was the captain, mate, cook, tackle expert and baby sitter.

I was shaking inside from anticipation. I wished that I could hurry Gainey up and get to the Tortugas now. I wasn't even sure Dawn and Limbo were still alive. I had to believe they were.

I went inside the cabin, untied the boy's shoes and removed them. I threw their socks in the corner of the boat, pulled out their shirt tails, an messed up their hairdos.

Mama began to say something but I interrupted.

"Boys, this is Florida! We have fun in Florida. You're not going to church out here. You're fishing."

I noticed their mom smile for the first time. I picked up a whole squid from the bait table and threw it at the boy on the left. It hit him, at his second button, leaving a nice little slime stain. He picked it up and slapped his brother upside the head. After a five minute exchange of squid tossing, everyone was laughing. Although I wanted to fire one in the direction of Dr. Dad, I decided not to.

I rigged up some light tackle and trolled four rods at a time. The day passed quickly. By the time we pulled in the lines and headed to the Tortugas, the two boys had caught kingfish, barracuda, wahoo and dolphin. More important, they had fun. I think this was the first time they had ever enjoyed just being kids. After the fishing, I stripped them down to their underwear and I shed my own clothes, leaving only my boxers. I took a bar of soap and lathered the three of us up. I then tossed the boys overboard, and dove in after them.

I had to almost force them back on the boat. After drying them off, their mom gave the two some fresh shirts. Both boys wrinkled up the shirts and slipped them on. Their feet stayed bare for the remainder of the trip.

In the forty-five minutes it took us to reach our destination, I was offered a job and a gracious tip. I told Captain Gainey I didn't need a job, but thanks anyway. I told the happy couple from New Jersey I surely didn't need any more money. They were surprised.

"But there is one thing you can do for me," I said. "Take care of those two boys, let 'em be kids, and tell them how much you love them, as often as possible."

They were now thinking my brain had been completely baked by the sun and that I was some sort of crazy. I didn't care. I'm from Florida.

When we approached the channel at Garden Key, we could see a melange of sea craft littering the harbor. From sailboats and sportfishers to sea planes, all were moored in areas on both sides of the narrow firth. With their anchor lines all aimed in the same direction, their sterns faced us as we slowly slipped through.

In one leap I made it from the flying bridge, down to the cockpit. As I covered my face, we passed within six feet of the *Gold Digger*. When I looked back at the boat, rocking slightly from our wake, I felt happiness as well as sadness. Sitting on the back of the boat were Limbo and Dawn with frozen drinks in hand. They were alive. They were talking and smiling. I felt good. On the bow, checking the anchor line was Gray's mate. I did not feel so good now. It was Jenny. Gray joined her, gave her a pinch on the butt and kissed her firmly. I turned and sat quietly for a moment. Captain Gainey pulled us up to the dock. While I tied the bow line to the cleat, he secured the stern. The *Look Out* had a permanent berth here at the only dock in the Dry Tortugas.

Captain Gainey was glad I had cleaned all the gear and re-rigged the tackle for tomorrow. Not only had I scrubbed the twins, but I had also washed down the boat. It met the Captain's standards.

"Just relax, Powell. You've done enough today. Besides, you're in for a treat," he said.

It turned out that Captain Gainey was a gourmet cook. At the end of each fishing day he would cook up a superb dinner using the days' catch.

With Mrs. Jersey lending a hand in the galley, I decided to look around the island.

"Mind if I go check out the fort before the sun goes down?" I asked.

"Be my guest. We eat in an hour," Gainey replied.

It took some talking to convince the twins that they did not want to accompany me. They liked their new friend from Florida.

Gainey said he wanted me to inspect the large trapezoidal fort on Garden Key so that I could better understand the story he would tell later. I wasn't sure what he meant, but I agreed.

I crossed over the small ten-foot bridge that spanned the width of the moat. It appeared that the entire fort was surrounded by a ten-foot wide, twenty-foot deep man-made canal. I climbed up on the brick wall and looked back at the harbor. Limbo and Dawn were still aboard the *Gold Digger*. Chef Gainey was chopping veggies and the two kids were flopping around in the water next the *Look Out*.

I jogged along the high wall looking for a particular red *Scarab*, go-fast boat. When I reached the back side of the island, I saw her. Sloan was anchored up all alone in the center of a huge gaggle of bird life. It was a sight that under different circumstances, I would have cherished. The movement and sounds of the twenty or thirty different species of birds seemed choreographed.

Even Sloan seemed to enjoy the movement as he sat lifelessly atop his starboard engine.

The sun was fading away quickly. I felt sure that Sloan and Gray would lay low for the evening. Tomorrow was the day they must have planned for the disappearance of Mrs. Adams.

I ran to the west side of the fort and sat down. The sun was a huge orange ball sinking quickly into the water. I missed the green flash. I continued along the wall until I had made a complete circle around the entire fort and island. I wondered how long it had taken to build the brick wall. It was at least fifty feet high and eight feet wide. The inside wall of the fort was a barricade built to keep those inside from escaping. Outside on the same wall, the bricks disappeared underwater forming one side of the moat. It was ingenious architecture for its time.

After completing my search of the area, I jumped down off the wall and headed back toward the *Look Out* to meet up with Captain Gainey.

When I passed the *Gold Digger*, I could see everyone inside her cabin. Limbo and Dawn sat at one side of the table. Gray and Jenny faced them. They were eating and laughing.

Gray and Jenny were good at this. If I hadn't known better, I'd have thought these two couples were best friends. Luckily, Limbo and Dawn were equally good actors .

When I boarded the *Look Out*, my eyes must have shown surprise. It looked as if someone had set up a photo shoot for a gourmet magazine. An aqua linen tablecloth covered the table. At each place was a pink linen napkin with sterling flatware tucked snugly inside. A bottle of wine was chilling in a flowery bucket of ice. There were crystal wine goblets next to each tea glass.

"Just in time, Powell. Clean up, it's all ready," Chef Gainey Maxwell barked.

As I washed my hands I thought maybe I shouldn't have taught the boys how to squid fight.

I sat between Mark and Mike as they requested. This time I remembered their names.

After the conch chowder and Caesar salad I ate three helpings of Mango Mahi-Mahi.

"I think this is the best meal I've ever eaten," said the doctor. We all agreed that Captain Gainey was a remarkable cook.

He had filleted the dolphin into strips three inches wide and ten inches long. After pan-frying them slightly, he poured fresh cut mangoes over the top and covered them to simmer in the juices for about five minutes. I'm not sure what else he did, but it was the tastiest mahi-mahi I ever ate. Gainey said he would write down the recipe. I couldn't wait to cook it for Dawn and the guys back at Coco's.

After all was cleaned up, Captain Gainey told everyone to get ready for story time. It was a little extra he threw in when kids were along. Mark and Mike went to the head. I went outside and glanced down the harbor. All was calm and I could still see Limbo and Dawn.

Everyone got comfortable in the spacious cockpit of he *Look Out*. Mark and Mike were both half in my lap. Captain Gainey Maxwell, the story teller, began his tale.

"Once upon a time, a long time ago, It was late night, April 14, 1865. Dr. Samuel Mudd was just finishing up some work and ready to head home to his wife. It had been a rough week and he had seen more patients than he cared to think about. In fact, his wife was a little upset with Ol' Sam because he was working so hard and unable to take her to the theater earlier that same evening. The play *Our American Cousin*, a comedy, was playing at the Ford Theater. Everybody that was anybody was there except Mrs. Samuel Mudd." The twins were all ears as the Captain continued.

"Just as Sam was starting to lock up, a man came shuffling through the front door with an obvious limp. A tired, dedicated physician, Dr. Mudd set the broken leg and finally headed home. He arrived home about one o'clock in the morning and was in the middle of explaining to his lovely spouse as to why he was so late, when the authorities came in and arrested him. He had not had a good day.

"The next morning he found out that the leg he had fixed belonged to John Wilkes Booth."

Mark, or maybe it was Mike, yelled out, "That's the man that killed President Lincoln. We're studying that in history."

"That's right," Gainey continued. "In fact, Dr. Mudd was arrested as a conspirator in the assassination of Abraham Lincoln. They put him on a ship headed for Charleston and told him he would stand trial and if found innocent would be set free. However, the captain of the vessel was told by authorities not to stop in Charleston, but to continue south to a rather grim prison on Garden Key in the Dry Tortugas.

"This is the very spot where Dr. Samuel Mudd arrived. He was imprisoned here at Fort Jefferson in 1865.

"After four long years, Dr. Mudd's heroic services to the sick and dying in a yellow fever epidemic won him his pardon in 1869.

"When he returned home, he found an empty house. His wife had left him. He lost his practice and all of his patients. To top it all off, the man whom he didn't even know and who caused all his grief, John Wilkes Booth, had been killed in a barn hideout only twelve days after Mudd had fixed his leg. The only good outcome of Dr. Samuel Mudd's life was that his story would remind people for generations on the importance of a good reputation. He is responsible for the old saying that we've all heard and probably didn't realize where it came from—'His name is Mudd!'"

"Guys, tomorrow you can go ashore and get some pictures of the fort. You can show your history teacher a few things you learned in the Tortugas."

I'm sure I enjoyed the story more than Doc and his family. The twins were about to fall asleep. I was so mesmerized I almost forgot my worries.

"Oh shit," I said without realizing it.

"What's wrong, Powell?" the Mrs. asked.

"I was supposed to call my father yesterday and let him know how I was doing. I'm afraid he'll worry about me."

Although that was the truth, it was not what I needed to do. I needed to flip the VHF back to channel 65 and call Customs.

I asked Captain Gainey if I could use the radio for a minute. He said, "Sure. "

I tried for twenty minutes to raise someone. No one listened from the other end.

When I returned, all were sleeping. I sat at the table and looked over some charts for the area.

The *Gold Digger* was anchored in the channel between Garden Key, the home of Fort Jefferson, and Bush Key. According to the chart, Bush Key was off limits this time of year, a time when noddy and sooty terns were nesting there. This was also the time loggerhead turtles laid their eggs in the sand on the keys around Fort Jefferson. I crawled into the only bed left, fading into the night, just as the sun had earlier.

My eyes opened early. It took only a few moments to locate myself. I looked at my watch. The first purchase using my new monies would be to replace this Seiko with another brand.

At three-forty a. m. in the Tortugas, the world was quiet. I silently went up top to look around and was surprised not only to see the lights on in the *Gold Digger*, but also that most of the boats that had been anchored here earlier had left.

There was no movement aboard Gray's boat. Things were too still. Something was wrong. I jumped on the wharf, ran down the beach and slipped quietly into the water. I swam out to the *Gold Digger* and eased myself aboard. It was deserted. They had abandoned ship in the middle of the night. Why I wondered? Where were Customs and the Coast Guard?

I quickly rummaged through the boat looking for a gun or weapon. All I could find was a fillet knife. I grabbed it, along with a flashlight and a pair of binoculars and I ran as fast as I could to the other end of the island. Sloan's boat had not moved. Even with the help of the binoculars I couldn't tell if he was aboard.

A noise got my attention. It came from Bush Key, an awful sound. The nesting birds were frantic. Something had interrupted their nesting plans. Then it hit me. Sloan was not aboard his boat. Where were the hundreds of birds that had surrounded his *Scarab* when I watched him earlier? Someone had spooked them, just as someone was now spooking the terns on Bush Key.

I did not use the flashlight in fear of making myself a human target. When I reached the channel, I swam it with ease. Once on Bush Key I sprinted down the beach toward the sounds of the irate birds. The sun would not rise for another hour and the only light cast in my path was from the last phase of the moon. As I neared the birds, I tripped on something, burying my face into the sand.

By reflex I hit the switch on the flashlight and aimed it at what had tripped me up. When I saw it, I turned off the light and jumped into the mangroves. It was Harrison Gray. His throat had been cut. He was lying on his back, eyes wide open, gazing upward toward the very birds that brought me to him. I could do him no good. He was quite dead.

I was about to desert Bush Key when I heard someone coming. I backed down into the mangroves as far as possible. I heard a voice that I recognized. It was Jenny.

"I'll bet the next time some girl asks you to take a romantic stroll along the beach, you'll think twice. Poor Harrison thought he was coming out here to get laid. Well I guess in a way, you got your wish," she said to the corpse.

"I only wish I had brought this shovel with us the first time. It's a long way back to the boat, Darling."

I hoped she would hurry. The sun's rays were beginning to bend over the horizon. I did not want to confront her yet.

She easily dug a hole in the sand, then rolled Gray over, face down, into his shallow grave and covered him. When she tossed the shovel, I had to duck to keep from being hit. She headed back toward the fort.

It was pretty smart to bury Gray here. Because of the hundreds of thousands of terns that nest on Bush Key, the place would be off limits for another two or three months. In a few weeks the birds, turtles, crabs, lizards, fiddlers and rats would surely pick the corpse clean.

When I arrived back at the channel, I saw Jenny's silhouette on top of the brick wall. As soon as she jumped down into the fort, I swam so fast I barely got wet. I hit the beach, ran to the wall and caught a glimpse of Jenny as she entered one of the cells on the bottom floor. The sun was up enough for me to see the *Look Out* as she idled out of the harbor. Today's fishing promised to be a little tougher on the captain—he had no mate.

Quietly I crept to the entrance of the cell and peered in, careful not to be seen.

There was no evidence of Sloan in the room when I showed up. Limbo and Dawn were tied up and sitting on the floor with their backs to me. Jenny was standing behind Dawn while talking to Limbo. I got as close as possible without being seen. Although I was only a few feet from Jenny, I felt helpless. My fillet knife was no match for the automatic weapon she carried.

"Well, Dr. Adams, it's time to grant you your wish. Was this trip worth seven hundred fifty thousand dollars, Doc? I certainly hope so, because I'm afraid it's going to be your last."

"Please don't kill her. She's not my wife," Limbo pleaded.

"No shit, Doc. Do you really think we're that stupid? Even with the makeup job, she looks nothing like the photo you gave us," Jenny said.

I was becoming very confused.

"You forgot, Dr. Adams. I was present on both times when you and your wife visited Caribbean Jewelers. I also surprised your wife as she stepped out of your dead friend's shower," she said laughingly.

"Dead? Powell's dead?" Limbo asked.

"Yeah, my ol' work buddy, had a terrible accident on the way out here to save you. That rented boat had a bad gas leak. When he tried to light his cigar, he blew himself into the ozone layer," Jenny said.

"Powell doesn't smoke," Limbo said.

"That's my story and I'm sticking to it," Jenny said, while laughing so hard, it made me ill.

Jenny then pressed her pistol to the back of Dawn's head and said, "Bye, bye Mrs. Adams."

I jumped out, ran toward Jenny and hit her on the back of the head with the butt end of the flashlight, knocking her out cold. At the same time a bullet pierced Dawn's skull.

As I grabbed Dawn's drooping head, I cried and screamed, "No! , No! When I looked into her eyes, I realized what Jenny and Limbo had been talking about. This poor, beautiful dead girl was not Dawn. I grabbed Jenny's gun, made sure she was still out cold and cut Limbo loose.

"I wanted to tell you, but I never saw you again to explain. After our meeting with Customs, I figured it was too dangerous for Dawn. This poor woman is, was rather, an undercover Customs agent. Jesus Christ," Limbo said as he checked her pulse. "I sure didn't want anything like this to happen, but we all knew it was possible. That's the reason Dawn is safe and sound back in Key West," Limbo said.

"Thanks, Limbo. I'm happy Dawn is OK. If I'm lucky maybe I'll get to see her soon," I said.

"Don't count on it, guys."

Limbo and I both turned to see who was talking. It was Sloan himself.

"Hey, boys," he said. "How's the fishing trip?"

I sensed movement behind me, but dared not turn and look.

"Look who's awake, guys," Sloan said.

"Jenny, would you please take your gun from Powell?" Sloan

continued.

"With pleasure," Jenny said as she bludgeoned the side of my skull with its butt.

I fell to the ground dazed. I tried hard to stay conscious and listen. I did not want to die. I wanted to see my family and Dawn. I hated the thought of dying for money.

I heard a scream, followed by rapid gunfire. Jenny fell beside me before the gun shots had stopped. This was a nightmare I wanted to end. Three people were dead and two more were about to join them. I looked over at Jenny. Her sad eyes were fixed on mine. I found the strength to stand. I stared at Sloan and asked him, "Why? Why are you killing everyone?"

"Powell, you don't seem to understand. I didn't kill these people. You and your accomplice here did. I loved Jenny, we were going to be married. I would never have hurt her," Sloan said with his usual snarl, and continued to tell us his devious plan. He said I had stolen three hundred thousand dollars worth of diamonds from him the day I was fired. He had reported it to the authorities immediately that day.

"That's bull shit and no one will believe that," Limbo said.

Sloan took an envelope out of his top pocket and emptied the contents on the floor by my feet. There were about fifteen large diamonds of all shapes and sizes.

"Oh, I think I'll be able to convince the police I'm right. I'll have plenty of time to place the blame for all these murders on you and your friend," Sloan said.

Jenny's lifeless body was at my feet. Four feet away was her pistol. With only three of us present, I looked at Limbo for guidance. He shifted his eyes to the floor, toward the weapon. I didn't give myself time to think of any consequences. For some unknown reason we had no back up, no Customs, no Coast Guard, and no choice. I jumped over Jenny's frail body, did a tuck and roll, kicking the gun in Limbo's direction. With the pistol sliding across the concrete slab, sounds from another blast of gunfire deafened me. I was trapped within my own small world. Though my eyes watched as Limbo retrieved the gun and jumped behind a column, there was no sound. Like watching a silent movie, I was only a spectator with my thoughts trapped between my ears. When my hearing finally returned, I heard Limbo yelling my name.

"Powell? Powell, are you OK?" I thought it an odd question, until I attempted to stand. The pain in my left calf forced me to look down. One of the many slugs spit from Sloan's automatic rifle had ripped through my leg, opening the flesh to the bone. I had seen month-old, ground hamburger meat in better condition. My heart was racing. Blood was pouring from the wound. There was no pain, but I couldn't stand. I was just checking to see if I had any feeling in my leg when Sloan's arm came from nowhere, locked around my neck and jerked me to my feet. I felt extreme pain, total body pain. My leg was on fire and the incessant tension on my throat was forcing an ugly world upon me.

My vision of Limbo was a little vague, slightly dreary. As I began to enter a dismal black hole in this universe, I felt my right hand fall to my side. From instinct only, I fumbled through my pocket finding the molded handle of the fillet knife I had earlier taken from the *Gold Digger*. I lifted the knife and rammed the six-inch stainless steel blade through the side of Sloan's neck. The pressure released on my throat. I heard one final gunshot as I fell to the floor spewing vomit through most of the room. I looked back over my shoulder. Sloan was stretched out flat on his back. With one eye he was staring in the direction of Key West. His other eye was missing. When Sloan felt the blade of my knife pierce his vocal cord, he dropped me. Before he could raise his rifle, Limbo put one bullet through Sloan's brain, right through his left eye socket.

With a half hug and half grab, Limbo lifted me to my feet.

When we walked through the narrow doorway of the cell's entrance, the warm sunlight felt good. The air was crisp and clear. Frigate birds glided on air currents above, watching over Garden Key.

Limbo looked deep into my eyes, winked, and said, "Shit!"

Neither one of us looked back into the room.

Chapter Sixteen——

Limbo and I sat on the beach and waited as our reinforcement arrived too late. A sea plane landed in the channel and beached itself fifty feet from us. The helicopter landed inside the fort. Six men wearing fatigues and carrying rifles fled from the plane, also disappearing inside the walls of the fort. Limbo shook his head in disgust. When Captain Coast Guard stepped out of the plane Limbo stood and motioned him over to us.

Before he really was close enough to carry on a conversation, Limbo yelled to him, "Where the fuck have you been, Captain?"

The captain's explanation was excusably believable. It seems that yesterday afternoon, about thirty minutes after I had called Customs from Captain Gainey's boat, they received another call. The caller, probably Sloan or Gray, identified themselves as Limbo. He told the authorities that nothing would happen until later. He then instructed them not to show up at the Tortugas until noon today, for fear of alerting the enemy.

I looked at my watch. It was twelve fifteen. I unstrapped the rubber band and threw the Seiko and all it represented, as far as I could. A few curious fish watched as it sank in the clear water between Garden and Bush Keys. The captain said he thought he was indeed talking to Limbo. For fear of tipping off Sloan he decided to wait as instructed. We said we understood. Limbo took two agents to the cell where Sloan and Jenny lay dead, while I produced Gray's body for the captain.

When we returned to the fort, the head of the Coast Guard told Limbo, "We'll be a day or so finishing up here, but I'll have one of the guys fly ya'll back to Key West. I have a few more questions for you so I'll get with you in a couple of days."

I had the helicopter pilot radio ahead to contact Dawn. I wanted her to know it was over and that Limbo and I had survived.

When we were landing in Key West, two huge DC-3's were dumping thousands of gallons of pesticides over the Salt Ponds south of the airport.

Limbo, pointed to the clumsy antique looking aircraft and said, "Hopefully, that's the only exterminator left in Key West now," he smiled and continued. "You did good, Powell."

"Thanks, Limbo."

Watching the plane dropping a deadly liquid in an effort to rid the island of those pesky mosquitoes reminded me once again of my dad. His last warning as I left home for the Keys was, "Stay away from Key West at night."

He honestly believed that mosquitoes were partly responsible for spreading the AIDS's virus. He thought that if a mosquito bit a person who was infected and then bit me, the HIV virus was sure to enter my blood stream. He compared the virus to malaria, when it took scientists years to realize it was a female mosquito that spread the disease. If only he knew what I had been through in the last twenty-four hours, I'm sure his mosquito phobia would have disappeared.

"I need to call him," I thought.

When we landed, Dawn was waiting at the gate. It's difficult to describe the feeling I had when I first laid eyes on her that day. The tearful reunion was one of happiness and sorrow. I was sad to have been away and for any worry I had caused her. I was glad to know that I would spend my life with this special lady.

After spending two hours at the hospital getting my leg tended, we dropped Limbo off and headed to Cudjoe.

The hot bath was nice, but what followed was delicious.

While laying on my back, Dawn slowly positioned herself above me. Her gold hair tickled the side of my neck as her warm breasts pushed against my chest. With slow gentle movements she alternated from sitting up on me to bending over and kissing my mouth. In all the times we would make love in our life I wondered how many times it would be like this.

I pulled Dawn into my arms. With our flesh one, I floated off into the night. The next morning we slept much later than normal.

It took a couple of months for me to dispose of my new money. I bought the *Gold Digger* at the Custom's auction rather cheaply. I purchased myself a new watch, a Swiss-made watch unlike my old Seiko.

I called Charles, Sr. and had him make Dawn a nice engagement ring with a two-carat emerald cut diamond in the center and a half carat trillion cut diamond on either side. He set it all in platinum. She loved it. She said yes, of course. The ring was as flawless as the beautiful lady that wore it.

I surprised Carlos and Flora by having central air put in Coco's Cantina. After all of my purchases I still had enough money to live comfortably for quite some time. Soon, I would take some time to fish with Limbo and Dawn.

One cool spring afternoon I invited some friends over for a taste of mango snapper. Gainey Maxwell, the old crusty captain came alone. Carlos, Flora and Dennie showed up early. Jeffrey and his family stopped by a little later.

When Limbo finally arrived, he was bearing a gift. A nice gift.

"Here, Powell. I want you to have this for the boat. It'll look good on the coffee table, and besides, I don't appreciate it like you do," he said as he handed me *The Reef*.

"Thanks, Limbo, you're a good friend. Hey buddy, maybe we ought to rename it. How about *The Deadly Reef*?" I said.

"How about *Reef Retired*," Limbo said laughingly.

I agreed.

As everyone was enjoying the meal, the phone rang.

"It's for you, Powell. It's your dad," Dawn said.

"Hey, Dad, what's up?"

"Your mother was worried about you. You know, being unemployed and not having an income we thought maybe we could help out," he said.

I thought it best not to tell him I had a thirty-eight foot boat, a house, a Maverick skiff, the *Reef Retired*, no bills, and nearly half-a-million dollars cash. He might not understand.

One day I would tell him the entire story of how Limbo and I pulled off the whole thing. I would tell him about the lady who had hired us and why I didn't need to work. Maybe by then the widow would have surfaced. For now it seems she had left the country with all of her inheritance. I figured Limbo had lied about her in an effort to ease my conscience. I never asked, because I never wanted to know for sure.

For now, both my financial status and the exact whereabouts of the widow would remain a secret.

"Dad, I appreciate the thought and thank Mom too, but I'll be OK. I'm gonna start guiding in a couple of weeks. Besides, I've got a little money saved up. You have nothing to worry about. My life here in the Keys with Dawn is great. And Dad, I want to tell you something I've been trying to say for years."

"What's that, Powell?" he asked.

"I love you, Dad."

There was a pause and then he said, "Uh, Powell why don't you and Dawn move back here to Gulf Breeze? You can help run the store, and ya'll could have a good life here."

"Not just yet, Dad," I said.

"OK, if you're sure," he replied. "Oh, and son, uh, um, I mean, If I can do anything at all for you, let me know. I, uh, um I, I'll see you soon, son. "

I knew what he meant and it felt good.